Thin Air

Thin Air

Gerald Hammond

St. Martin's Press
New York

M

Library of Congress Cataloging-in-Publication Data

Hammond, Gerald.
    Thin air / Gerald Hammond.
      p.   cm.
    ISBN 0-312-11339-0
    1. Calder, Keith (Fictitious character)—Fiction. I. Title.
PR6058.A55456T48   1994
823'.914—dc20   94-32248
                                          CIP

First published in Great Britain by Macmillan London Limited a division of Pan Macmillan Publishers Limited

First U.S. Edition: December 1994
10 9 8 7 6 5 4 3 2 1

ONE

I was at my desk, looking south past the blank screen of the word processor and across farmland which glowed and shimmered in the bright July sunshine. The scene represented some of the best of the Scottish Borders, fertile and ripening and punctuated by trees in full leaf; but the hills in the distance were England, still in some ways my spiritual home. I had come to love Scotland and I knew that much of the England of my youth had vanished under feet and Tarmac. But as long as there is life in the plant it is the roots that survive.

The fine weather was calling me into the great outdoors. I had been doodling, writing nothing in particular in the hope that something would take shape. Triggered by the sight of a couple dallying in the fields, I had wondered idly why there were exactly two sexes throughout nature. Leaving aside the amoeba, the invertebrate hermaphrodites and certain plants, higher up the evolutionary ladder there was never but one; and except for the uncertain example of the bees and their relatives, never three. I find an evolutionary explanation of the universe perfectly satisfying, but why had the process of evolution ordained that multisexual species should fail – or perhaps never have been tested?

Great ideas sometimes spring from such whimsical beginnings. I would rather have gone to sit in the garden for a period of toying with the thought, but Alice, who would have fought like a tigress to prevent anyone from interrupting me at my desk, could never understand that a writer may still be working while wandering around the house with a glazed expression, muttering to himself, or slouched, apparently somnolent, in a deckchair in the garden. My appearance on the lawn would have been an immediate signal for 'Run along and play with your dad,' and, dearly as I love our children in small- to medium-sized doses, a boy of six (or possibly seven, I could never remember) and a three-year-old girl are not ideal companions while gestating a book or groping in the recesses of the mind for the seeds of a new one.

Alice, by the way, was and is my wife, despite rumours to the contrary. When she first moved into Tansy House with me, ostensibly as my housekeeper, she made it clear that, while I would never pass for a Scot, she had no intention of letting me marry her until I could at least pass among the Scots without laying myself open to ridicule. I accepted the situation, largely because it slotted well into the tax regulations then in force.

With the passage of time I became accepted as mildly eccentric but a part of the local scene, but long before then we were recognized as a more or less married couple and Alice was invariably addressed as Mrs Parbitter. With an extension of her inverted feminine logic, she then explained that nothing would induce her to admit publicly that we had been cohabiting and we therefore sneaked off for à secret wedding from my cousin's house in the Lothians – with the inevitable result that we were generally believed still to be living in sin.

The arrival at the front gate of a vehicle promised a welcome respite. The basket behind me creaked as Boss, my elderly Labrador, recognized the beat of the engine and raised his head. I got up and hurried out before Alice could send the visitors packing.

From my window my view of the vehicle had been cut off

by the hump of rockery separating Tansy House from the narrow road. Now, from my higher viewpoint, it looked very like the jeep belonging to the Calder family. But Keith, I knew, had gone south with his wife and married daughter to spend three days at the Game Fair.

Heads began to appear as I descended the steps. Keith might be away in the family car but his jeep was still around. All three occupants were connected to him. The driver, a thin man with a full head of greying hair and a serious expression, was Wallace James, Keith's partner in the gunshop. The large and rough-hewn man in hairy tweeds was Ronnie, Keith's brother-in-law. And climbing with difficulty out of the back was Ian Fellowes, who was both Keith's son-in-law and a CID Inspector. (The arrival of the local CID chief failed to worry me. The post was usually almost a sinecure. Ian dealt faithfully with the minor crimes that occur in any rural division. Anything more serious brought down the bigger wheels from Edinburgh and Ian was relegated to the position of supplier of local knowledge and liaison man with the uniformed branch.)

'Coffee or beer?' I asked. 'Or a dram?'

'A dram,' Ronnie said predictably.

But Wallace shook his head. 'Thanks,' he said, 'but we've just had. We're here to ask if you'd like to come rabbiting.'

'Failing which,' Ian said when I showed surprise, 'Boss. Keith took his dogs to the Game Fair with him and we don't have a decent retriever between us.'

All was now clear. I did not and do not shoot. I have come to terms with the need to control rabbits, pigeon and corvids although something in me recoils from the act of killing. But I had inherited Boss as a trained gundog. I had kept up his training because he seemed to enjoy it, and I had even worked him at picking up on the local shoots, which I justify to myself as an act of mercy in preventing pricked birds escaping to suffer.

'Boss wouldn't want to go without me,' I said. This was clearly untrue. Boss was frisking around his old friends and sporting companions like a young pup. 'Come in while I fetch my boots.'

'C-catch us up,' Wallace said. He has an occasional nervous stammer which disappears as he settles down. 'We're only going to Easter Coullie.' He nodded to where, beyond the road and a few fields, the buildings of Easter Coullie Farm fitted comfortably into the landscape. 'Keith's syndicate is the shooting tenant. Old Murdo says that if we don't do something about the rabbits he'll let somebody else in.'

'And that could be any poaching bugger,' Ronnie added.

'Don't start without me,' I said, and they squeezed themselves back into the small vehicle.

Easter Coullie would be dry in such weather. Leather boots would do, rather than Wellingtons. I changed my footgear, grabbed a thumbstick and told Alice where we were off to. Rather than take the nearly new BMW onto farmland, I set off on foot with Boss trotting happily at my heel. The old boy knew that an outing, when he had already had his morning stroll, and especially when preceded by a visit from several of his shooting acquaintances, presaged an emergence from limbo and a few hours of return to glorious life.

Cutting across a field containing some sheep which Boss treated as invisible, I vaulted a fence and followed the unsurfaced farm road towards the stone gable of a large barn. The road jinked slightly, left and then right, into a large farmyard which lay between the open front of the barn and the gable of a traditional farmhouse. The barn was backed by a tractor shed and a mini-labyrinth of other farm buildings in stone and slate. Most were in a good state of repair although I could see grass in the gutters.

As we rounded the corner of the barn, with my mind on

the shooting to come, I heard a bang above my head and I jumped and dropped my thumbstick. 'Sorry,' said a voice. Boss was peering round, looking for something to retrieve.

I looked round and up. Planks on trestles blocked half the open front of the barn. Duggie Bracken, the local joiner and Jack-of-all-trades, was up there beside what seemed to be a new steel girder spanning the front of the barn and his van was tucked inside with its doors open. He pulled off his ear protectors.

'I thought I'd been shot,' I told him.

'Well, you're no',' he said. The smile was missing from his habitually cheerful face. He had done some work at Tansy House and usually bubbled with good humour. 'It was only the Hilti spit-gun.'

I raised a hand in forgiveness and farewell and walked on. The jeep, I could see, had been driven through the farmyard and stopped a few yards up the rough farm track that continued south between the fields.

There was a small car in the yard, far from new, painted a pink which verged on the indecent, but lovingly polished. The tenant farmer, Old Murdo as he was always known, to distinguish him from his second son, was beside the gate to the walled garden of the farmhouse. He was conversing in low tones with a stout, blonde woman whom I had consulted once about Boss's ageing pains and had often seen in that or a similar car, tearing around the country roads with a mad, whirring sound.

(Alice, on reading the above words, remarked that no doubt the car had also been making odd noises. Alice never did take to Jean Mather. Not many did.)

Old Murdo Heminson had always been a cantankerous individual, quick to defend what he regarded as his rights, and it seemed to me that he had been getting worse of late. He broke off to shout at me. 'Hey! You! Where you taking yon dug?'

His square face was set in an ugly frown which was lent emphasis by his bad colour.

'To join the rabbiting party,' I said, and I walked on quickly past him. Old Murdo's temper was notorious and when the black mood was on him he was best avoided.

My answer had only partially deflated him. 'Keep the bugger awa' fae my yowes, or else. You hear me?'

I refused to kowtow to him but I was not going to provoke a shouting match. I let my head bob in a faint suggestion of a nod and kept walking. He turned back to the woman. 'The beast died,' I heard him say, 'and you can hae me afore the shirra, gin you're so minded. I'm no' payin' you to let my cattle die. Now go an' see to that yowe, an' if you make a job o't I'll maybe pay you for that.'

Bullying tactics towards the local professionals were unlikely to stand him in good stead, but it was no business of mine. I hurried out of earshot, towards the narrow end of a long rape-field almost ready for cutting. The yellow flowers had brought us an illusion of sunshine during the spring.

The jeep was parked in an open space where a second track ran off to the west, giving access to the south side of the farm buildings and some further fields. The rabbiting party was unsleeving guns and donning cartridge belts. Ronnie was transferring ferrets into a carrying box.

'It's the wrong time of year for ferreting, isn't it?' I asked curiously. No information is ever superfluous to a writer.

'I wouldn't put 'em down a burrow,' Ronnie said. 'They'd kill underground and stay down. It's the cowps of stones we've to clear. They'll not have young in there. Too cold. Here, you'll be needing a wipe of this.' He handed me a jar of insect repellent cream. 'There's clegs and a' damn thing where we're going.'

A cleg is a horsefly and its bite can go septic. I smeared the cream liberally over my exposed surfaces.

8

'Your job,' Wallace said, 'with Boss, is to stop them bolting back among the stones we've just cleared.'

I had worked that ground with Keith in the past and knew it for difficult territory. 'What about the holes?' I asked. 'The banking's riddled with them.'

'Never heed them,' Ronnie said. 'Young Murdo will be following behind us with the gas.'

There was a moment's hiatus. I had come to terms with the shooting of rabbits, over dogs or ferrets or by stalking, each of which methods demands fieldcraft by the hunter and gives the rabbit a sporting chance of escape. Gassing underground is a nasty business. Sometimes necessary but always nasty. I think that the others felt the same.

'Well, at least we won't have to worry if we shoot a few milky does,' Ian said. 'The young won't be left to starve. Who's that in the farmyard with Old Murdo? A fat woman with a pink car?'

'The vet's new assistant,' Wallace said. 'Not his usual style.' The local vet, a widower, was noted for choosing young and attractive females to assist him. Somehow they never stayed for very long.

'Old Murdo was refusing to pay a bill when I went by,' I said. 'Something to do with a beast that died.'

'He was coughing up a cheque to Duggie as we passed,' said Ian, 'and not looking too happy about it. I suppose the poor woman got the backlash. She'll send her boss to sort him out. Everyone set?'

Ronnie handed me his gun, picked up the ferret box and led the way south along the track away from the farm buildings, between a large field of barley and a pasture containing young bullocks. The barley was separated from the rape by a windbreak hedge where blackbirds sometimes nested. When I looked over my shoulder I could see Young Murdo plodding after us, carrying a spade and a sack.

Close to the farm boundary a stream had cut a wide arc through the land. The stream itself was modest, but I had seen it rise in spate after heavy rains. It had made a small gully for itself, varying from thirty to sixty feet wide and ten feet deep at the most, fringed on both sides by occasional trees. Beyond the stream the further embankment, which rose up to the boundary fence, was scarred with rabbit holes.

A cock pheasant was pacing along beside the stream. Ronnie waved his hat at it. 'Awa' back where you belong,' he said. The bird looked at him with disdain and then took off, whirring up and over the boundary.

'Why bother?' I asked. 'Keith has the shooting here.'

'Och, we don't shoot Easter Coullie more than once or twice a year. It's not worth the argy-bargy with Old Murdo. We pay him for the shooting rights to stop him letting them to any other bugger. He'd be just as likely to plant artichokes along the boundary to draw our birds across.'

The gully, which was bright with wildflowers, could have been a beauty spot except that for generations the stones uncovered in the fields, ranging from the size of a man's head up to that of a water-butt, had been tipped over the nearer edge until some of the mounds almost reached the level of the surrounding land. When our heads topped the rise, the flat bed of the gully had seemed to move as rabbits bolted, some to the holes in the bank and others into the piles of boulders. The barley crop was sparse and stunted for fifty yards out from the gully, clearly marking the territory where the rabbits fed.

Talk had ceased and we were moving quietly. Rabbits will sometimes stay and take their chance with the ferret rather than bolt if there has been too much disturbance above ground. Ronnie took his gun from me and pointed to the left. Boss followed me a little way down the valley to where our presence would deter any escape into some rough ground beyond.

Rabbits could have avoided a single ferret for hours in the myriad passages below the big stones. Ronnie put all four of his jills in and then took his place. The three men were all on the first heap of stones, facing outwards. They had worked as a team before. Young Murdo arrived and joined me in silence. He took an air rifle out of his sack, cocked and loaded it. I saw Ian, the nearest of the Guns, take note of our position and I gave him a wave.

'Your dad's on the rampage this morning,' I said quietly.

I rather liked Young Murdo and I think that he liked me. He was certainly more prepared to pass the time of day with me than he was with most others. Some considered him dour but I had only found him solemn and somewhat introspective. Unlike his father, he had seemed rather happier on the few recent occasions when I had bumped into him. But this was not one of his most cheerful days.

'When was he ever not?' he said glumly.

'He's been getting on at you, has he?'

'You could say that.'

The still scene suddenly came to life. The first rabbits bolted and there was a flurry of shots. Then all was quiet again. The rabbits were warned and the ferrets would be having to work hard to push them out.

One rabbit was hard hit but alive, jumping and squirming in the grass. I was about to send Boss for it so that I could administer the *coup de grâce*, regardless of risk to him from any more shots, but Young Murdo fired once with his air rifle. The sound was insignificant after the slamming of the shotguns, but the rabbit jumped once and lay still, about twenty yards from us.

'I can't abide to see anything suffer,' he said quietly.

'And you a farmer's son?' I said.

He frowned. He was only about sixteen, I judged – a stocky youth with a gentle face below curly hair which had obviously been cut at home. 'I make it easy for them, if I can. There's no need for cruelty.'

I nodded my heartfelt agreement. 'It was a good shot,' I said.

'I can kill them dead at three times the range when I want.' The effect was spoiled by a huge yawn. I took the boast with a pinch of salt. I may not know much about guns, but I had had an airgun in my youth and sixty yards is a very long shot.

The ferrets seemed to have pushed the rabbits to the far end of the stones. Ronnie and Wal were shooting steadily but Ian was being left out of the action.

'I'm surprised you don't have a shotgun,' I told Young Murdo.

His frown became a scowl. 'Dad won't hear of it.'

The shooting ceased. One by one the ferrets surfaced and were gathered. Boss did his share of the picking up, his tail beating like a metronome. Eleven rabbits were gutted and hung in a handy tree to cool and the shooters moved on a hundred yards to where the next dump of rocks leaned against the slope. I washed my hands in the stream – I had no objection to dealing with the meat once it was deceased. The water was delightfully cool. Boss and I stood guard over the stone pile that had already been cleared.

The second heap of stones produced only one undersized rabbit but at the third, the largest of the lot and spread over fifty yards of banking, the shooting went on and on as the ferrets cleared passage after passage. When I looked back, Young Murdo had fallen far behind us. I could still see him, wearing a mask and gloves, spooning Cymag down each hole, filling in the hole quickly with earth and stamping it down. Cyanide gas is not to be trifled with. From time to time he glanced up at a small knoll which marked where the boundary turned away from the gully. From my window, I had sometimes seen a girlish figure lingering on the knoll. Perhaps Young Murdo's recent cheerfulness was explained.

We gutted another twenty rabbits, hung them on the fence and then took a seat by the stream, partly to cool off but also to give the ferrets a rest. Ian was slapping at the midges, which seemed to ignore the repellent.

'Take your boots off and have a paddle,' Wal told him. 'If you cool your blood down they'll leave you alone. Not you, Ronnie, or you'll kill the trout.'

Ronnie refused to be riled. 'I'll eat the fish if you won't,' he said.

We all dangled our bare feet in the stream and, as Wallace had predicted, the midges lost interest in us.

I heard a tractor go by and a little later I saw Brett, the older son, talking to Young Murdo. Reluctantly, for the day was humid and we were beginning to tire, we resumed our boots and prepared to move on. I was not looking forward to carrying the bag back to the car – rabbits in bulk can be very heavy. But the tractor arrived on the bank above us. Brett jumped down.

'I'll drop these off at your car,' he said. 'I've got your first lot.'

'Right,' Wal said. 'Thanks.'

Brett looked at us uncertainly. He was a more mature version of his brother. 'Dad's in a right temper today,' he said at last. No answer was called for. He looked from one to the other of us. 'Have you spoken with my brother?'

'I have,' I said.

'Did he answer you?'

'He wasn't his usual self,' I said. I remembered the yawn. 'He seemed sleepy.'

Brett nodded sombrely. By reputation he was a caring person and he seemed genuinely concerned for his younger brother. 'He was out half the night. Dad gie'd him laldie. A leathering,' he added to me in explanation. I had come to understand a large part of the Scots vocabulary but the locals still tended to interpret their own words for me. 'He had a go at me an' a'. But I can stand up for mysel'. I'm used to it.

Young Murdo was Dad's favourite at one time and he's taking it bad. Wouldn't say hardly a word to me. Keep an eye on him and if you get a chance try to cheer him up a bittie.' He turned away and collected our rabbits from the fence. I heard the tractor moving away.

'Why would the young devil be out half the night?' Ian wondered aloud.

'What do you think?' Wal retorted.

I nodded. 'Silly question,' I said. It must have been Young Murdo's figure that I had seen walking in the fields, and with the pretty daughter from the neighbouring farm.

'Aye,' Ronnie said. 'I'll bet my boots that's it.'

'No bets,' Ian said.

'You know I've the right of it?'

'No. But I've seen your boots.'

Ronnie only laughed. With strangers he would have flared up, but among friends he never seemed to mind being the butt. When he cared to make the mental effort he could give as good as he got.

The heat and closeness were exhausting. While the ferrets were clearing the next rock-pile, I slipped again into a reverie bordering on a doze. There might be a sci-fi book in my morning thought. A planet where there were three sexes. A could fertilize B, B could impregnate C but C could only couple with A. Some special term would be needed, to describe the orgy when all three matings took place simultaneously. A triang-bang, I wondered?

A single shot called me back to reality. A rabbit rolled over, recovered and bolted towards us, swerving towards the bank when it saw me. Boss, miraculously rejuvenated, intercepted it and brought it, squirming, to my hand. I gave it the quietus with a staghorn priest that I had found among my uncle's belongings. I could have broken its neck by hand, but not without suffering the mental shudders.

14

I glanced back over my shoulder. Young Murdo was still hard at work. During our respite he had almost caught up with us, but we were moving steadily upwind so I guessed that we were in no danger from the gas. When he saw me watching he raised a hand. I decided that he was not likely to put his head down a rabbit hole and take a deep breath. Young love provides a remarkably good incentive for remaining alive.

The breeze was bringing with it a strong smell, reminding me that we were arriving at the nearest point of the stream to the farm buildings where an enormous tank, walled and floored with concrete, was sunk into the ground. This, Keith had said, was originally intended for silage, but it had been made obsolete by the new silo that now reared above the skyline like a Martian invader. It was used instead by the farmer as a midden or slurry tank to hold his winter's accumulation of dung. The smell seemed to excite the midges. Other flies came to drink our sweat.

The passing of the tractor above us was a welcome distraction from the smell. Here, the stream was no longer on the boundary. The side-track between the farm buildings and the edge of the rape-field rose to cross the gully by way of an old stone bridge, in order to serve a couple of Easter Coullie fields beyond. The bridge was humped high over a generous arch, to allow for spates which could be strong when snow was melting on the hills.

Apart from the sporadic shooting, the morning had been peaceful, but now we became aware of shrill noises from the track. Guns and ferret-box were laid aside and we climbed the bank.

The vet's pink car was stopped, facing the bridge and the farm buildings. Miss Mather and Brett stood beside it. The tractor was parked nearby.

The woman was emitting high pitched screams and swinging an occasional punch at the young man. Such is the power of suggestion that I mistook the scene at first for one of assault or even rapine. As I came nearer, I realized that the screams were of laughter. Later, I remembered that her favourite gesture of affection was a punch to the upper arm – or to a more tender area if you were unlucky enough to be specially favoured.

Brett turned to meet us as we arrived. 'Miss Mather's car won't start,' he said. All five looked at me hopefully. My reputation as a mechanic with a magical touch, which derived from my having once co-authored a book about the tuning of racing motorcycles by a top mechanic, was greatly exaggerated and becoming a damned nuisance. The local black leather brigade often asked me to wave a magic wand over their motorbikes and were inclined to become aggressive when I was unable to help.

I looked at the car. It happened that one of my former girlfriends had owned a similar small DAF. 'It's only a six-volt system,' I said. 'But you could risk giving her a jump-lead start from the tractor.'

Brett shook his head. 'Battery's all right,' he said. 'It's the starter that's knackered. And it's no good pushing. It's automatic.'

'And here's me already late for my next appointment,' Miss Mather said cheerfully and waited for the big, strong men to do something clever and solve her problem for her. She was a competent vet but not very bright outside her profession, one of the many and surprising examples of the triumph of training over vacuity. Her head was covered with tight, blonde curls and she wore a sweater and trousers unsuitably close-fitting for her overblown figure. She was also sweating pro-fusely, attracting more than her fair share of the flies.

'If it gets up to a good speed, that'll turn the engine,' I said. 'We could push you to the top of the hump. It should start on the run down to the farm.'

Miss Mather turned to Brett. 'Why did you not think of

16

that?' she demanded, aiming a punch which he side-stepped. 'Come away, chiels. Give us a wee dunch.'

The faces of the men suggested that they would rather have pushed her into the nearest ditch, but we got behind the small car. Young Murdo arrived to add his weight. Miss Mather hopped into the driving seat. From the safety of the verge, Boss made noises that I took to be of encouragement.

The car moved easily at first, but the slope became steeper just before the hump of the bridge. We slowed and stopped.

'Handbrake,' Ian croaked.

'No' workin',' she said.

'You'll have to get out and help us,' I said.

She got out, slamming the door, and the car began to move again. We made a space for her. When she leaned her considerable weight against the back of the car it sailed easily up to the crest.

'In you get,' I said. 'Stick it in forward gear. Don't forget to turn on the ignition.'

'It's still on.' We were already over the crest and she had to hurry to reach the driver's door. 'I've locked myself out,' she said, laughing. 'Aren't I silly?'

We were now straining to hold the car back. 'The key,' I grunted.

'It's inside . . .'

'Put something solid under one of the wheels,' Ronnie told her.

'Like what?'

'Like your head,' Brett gasped.

She rounded on him. 'You've no call to talk to me like that, Brett Heminson,' she said.

Brett straightened up to face her, letting go of the back bumper. Ronnie had already turned aside to look for a large stone. My feet began to slide and I lost my grip. The others hung on for a few paces, but they too had to let go.

17

We ran after the car, but it soon outpaced us.

I had been right on one point. Evidently she had left the car in gear. When it was halfway down the slope we heard the engine fire.

TWO

At first, the car went straight down the middle of the track, guided by the ruts of a thousand journeys of tractor and trailer. It came to a slight kink as it neared the farm buildings and began to make the turn. A pothole in the track caused a lurch and I saw the wheel turn as though some driver were steering with malicious intent. With uncanny accuracy the car headed for the former silage pit. It had lost the thrust of the slope and was slowing, but not enough.

The little DAF seemed to hesitate on the brink, then skated onto the surface of the dung and slowly began to settle. Some recent rain had brought the upper layers of the dung to the consistency of thick porridge. The engine was still ticking over and the exhaust made a farting noise under the liquid manure. We gathered nearby. It had come to rest close to one side of the tank. I could have stepped onto its roof had I wished. A billion flies, disturbed from whatever it is that flies do in dung during hot weather, formed a dense cloud above it.

Disaster can attract a crowd even on a desert island. Alerted by the disturbance, Old Murdo joined us and stood leaning on his stick. He looked as sour as ever but I had a feeling that he was delighted to be on the scene of calamity. Other figures were following us over the bridge.

'Well, there's a pretty thing,' Miss Mather said shakily.

'Where?' said Young Murdo.

His father aimed a swipe at him with his stick but the boy jumped back.

Miss Mather was too preoccupied with her own troubles to pay much attention to anyone else. 'What'll you do?' she asked plaintively.

None of us answered her. My mind, I discovered, had gone blank. The whole episode was outwith the span of my thinking.

Old Murdo brought his mind back to the more immediate problem and I thought that he brightened. Retribution could wait. There was more fun to be had with Miss Mather. 'You did the business?' he asked her.

For a moment she gave precedence to her professional duties. 'Yes. You were right, the ewe's leg was broken. I put it down. There was nothing else to be done. What are we—?'

'You used an injection?'

Miss Mather shook her curls. 'I used the captive bolt humane killer. I knew you'd want to eat the meat. My car—?'

'I could howk it out for you,' Old Murdo said.

'Oh, please do,' said Miss Mather.

'I'll have to break some glass.'

'If you must.' The car lurched and settled another few inches. The hot exhaust was generating an incredible stink. 'But please hurry!'

He turned and stumped away. I wondered what on earth he thought he was going to do. I was soon enlightened. He returned from the tractor shed at the wheel of the large diesel fork-lift which was used for handling the big straw bales. For the only time in my experience of him, he looked happy. He lined the fork-lift up, one fork pointing at the rear window and the other at the driver's.

Miss Mather began to protest but the diesel was noisy and Heminson Senior was either unable or unwilling to hear. The two windows shattered. The diesel engine barked more loudly as the forks took the strain.

I expected the roof to be torn off, but the Dutch had built a solid little car. It deformed. The windscreen and the back window fell out. But it remained in one piece and slowly it came up as the dung released its hold. It was two-tone now, pink above and greenish brown below. One of the doors had come open and liquid dung was oozing out. Old Murdo turned the fork-lift and lowered the car. He stepped down and waited – for thanks or recriminations, I could not be sure.

Miss Mather, for once, seemed bereft of words. We stood and looked at the car. All that could have been said in its favour was that the engine was still running. It was a revolting sight. The forks had pushed the roof up into two large, pink humps.

'It looks exactly like a bum,' said Young Murdo thoughtfully, and I saw that it was so.

I was not sure whether the remark was intended as a frank comment or as an innocent joke aimed at relieving the tension. True or not, the comment was both tactless and ill-timed. His father rounded on him and lifted his stick again. I thought that the blow was no more than a gesture, not intended to land. But again the boy jumped back. As Old Murdo brought his stick round again in a backhanded swing, Brett pushed between them and took the blow across the face.

It was not in Old Murdo's nature to apologize, especially to one of his own sons. His pudding face was screwed up as though in pain and I took it for a sign of concern. Before he could speak, Brett jerked the stick out of his father's hand.

For ten tense seconds, real violence was in the air. I saw Ronnie braced to throw himself into the fray, as peacemaker on one side or the other, and Ian was putting on his policeman's face. Then Brett tried to break the stick across his knee. The heavy stick refused to break, so he tossed it into the dung.

We waited for all hell to break loose.

Then Brett swayed. Young Murdo grabbed him and pulled him away.

23

'Aye,' said their father hoarsely. 'Keep the sheepshank out of my sight.'

The figures that I had seen coming over the bridge had resolved themselves into Ken McKee, the neighbouring farmer, leaning on a stick even heavier than Old Murdo's, with his daughter Sheila. They had joined the throng during the extraction of the car. Brett was seated by the track, nursing his face. Young Murdo knelt beside him, but I intercepted a look that passed between him and the girl. There had been bad blood between the two farmers for as long as I had been in the district, much of it centering on the two Easter Coullie fields that obtruded into the McKees' land. It seemed that their progeny, far from continuing the quarrel, were in the early stage of falling in love.

'What's the old fool done to your bonny wee car?' McKee asked of Miss Mather.

She was waving her hands, less in despair than to ward off the flies. 'You've eyes in your head,' she said.

'I have. And if you want to go after him for damages, we're witnesses.'

'Och, I've no time for the likes of that,' Miss Mather said.

'If you change your mind . . .'

Old Murdo squared up to him. 'You'd like that fine, you bugger,' he said. 'But it's not up to Miss Mather. And her insurers'll not want to throw good money after bad. So you can tak' your ill-will back to your own ground and use it for the dung that's all it's fit for.'

McKee looked amused but his face had flushed. 'I've been shooting crows all morn,' he said, 'and any one of them was a better farmer than you. I'd go back for my rifle, forbye you're not worth the same bullet as a crow.'

Old Murdo was working himself up into a pitch of fury but he evidently felt that such insults as he had so far found fell short of the required standard. He glared at his younger son, still kneeling a few yards away. 'And as for you, you can stay away from that wee whore for good and all.'

Young Murdo flinched, either at the word or the embargo. 'Dad!'

'I mean it.' Old Murdo's face was screwed up with venom. 'No good'll come of your trailing a wing wi' the likes of her. Find yoursel' a decent lass from a good family and forget about this trasherie.'

Ken McKee gobbled for a few seconds but wisely decided against either violence or a slanging match. He took his daughter by the arm. 'That goes for you too,' he said grimly. 'If you so much as speak to that lout again, I'll have the skin off your back.'

The girl looked back as she was half led, half dragged towards the bridge. Young Murdo was staring after her as though he could pull her back by sheer willpower.

'You twa,' Old Murdo said, 'get back to your work. Brett, fetch back that carcase to the meat-shed.'

Brett got shakily to his feet. Young Murdo looked anxiously at the swelling that was rising on his brother's face but Brett nodded, clapped him on the shoulder and then hurried back to the tractor. I saw that he was limping from the blow he had given himself in his vain attempt to break his father's stick. Young Murdo walked off and disappeared into the valley.

Old Murdo returned his attention to Miss Mather and her car. 'There's a power-hose by the house,' he said gruffly. 'I'll put your wee car down there.'

Miss Mather humphed. 'I'd sooner drive it,' she said. 'I'm o'er late already. My partner'll be thinking something's happened. I was meant to meet him an hour back.'

The DAF's engine was still ticking over. She reached in through a glassless window, unlocked the driver's door and put the gear selector to neutral. Old Murdo backed the forklift clear. She tossed the windscreen into the back and carefully

25

removed some broken glass from the seat before getting in. She intended a disdainful expression but she only managed to look bilious.

The excitement seemed to be over. After some mutterings which might have been of excuse or apology, and before Miss Mather could find adequate reply, we turned away and started back towards the valley, walking quickly.

'They hate each other, the two daft buggers,' Ronnie said, 'but they needn't take it out on the youngsters. It's no' right. Yon Sheila's a good lass. Some day, that two could be well suited.'

I looked over my shoulder to see Miss Mather drive off. The car was deformed. It travelled slightly crabwise, leaving behind it a trail of dung and pulling a comet-like tail of flies, but it seemed to be running adequately. I wondered how Miss Mather's partner would react to being met with it.

We moved on. Beyond the bridge, we arrived at the last of the heaps of stones. When shooting finished, we had another dozen or so rabbits and only three or four more to clean. The other men had their knives out. I hung the already legged rabbits over my thumbstick and put it on my shoulder. 'I'll start back to the car with these,' I said.

Ronnie raised a bloodstained thumb to me.

The head of the gully was only a hundred yards or so from the nearer farm buildings but part of the rape-field lay in between. I could have returned to the bridge but, rather than face the smell and be reminded of the tragi-comedy when Miss Mather's DAF had taken its swim, or of the even less savoury behaviour of the two farmers, it seemed preferable to cross the pasture and rejoin my morning's route.

I could hear Duggie Bracken banging away. As the farmyard came into view Old Murdo appeared from the direction of the house. He seemed to have found another stick to walk with.

26

He gave me a glare which I could feel from a hundred yards away and checked in his stride, but he could see that Boss was tight at my heel and the sheep were quite undisturbed, so he walked on in the general direction of the jeep and passed out of my sight.

The day had become still and more humid and the sun seemed to be focused on me. I was sweating and beginning to hobble under the weight of the rabbits. Flies were determined to sample the rabbits' blood on my hands. Miss Mather and her car were out of my sight behind the house, but I could hear the whirr and swish of the power-hose and see an arc of rainbow. The spray looked invitingly cool and I decided, at the risk of being made the recipient of Miss Mather's complaints and tears or even being pressed into service, to bathe my hands and face.

I had almost made it to the corner of the barn when Mrs Heminson erupted from the back door of the house. She was the one member of the family whom I had not met, but I knew her by sight – a mountainous woman, a foot taller than her husband and twice his girth, with a face that had once been handsome but now sagged with jowls. By reputation, she had a tongue like a whip dipped in acid, but it was said that despite, or perhaps because of, their common mistrust of the rest of humanity, not excluding their own sons, they were a united and even devoted couple.

Her usual pace was a ponderous plod, but I saw that she was moving for once at a rapid trot. I could almost believe that I felt the ground shake. As she vanished beyond the barn, she uttered a cry that made the hairs crawl up the back of my neck. I nearly turned back, but curiosity spurred me on.

I rounded the barn.

Beyond the further end of it, not far from the jeep and only a few yards from the gate to the walled garden of the house, Old Murdo was lying on his back on the hard ground. His

27

wife was down on her knees, pulling at him and slapping at his face. Then, quite suddenly, she collapsed across him.

I dropped the rabbits, half glad of the excuse to get rid of the stick which was digging into my shoulder, and hurried closer. Old Murdo showed no signs of life. If he was not already dead, he was unlikely to last long with that weight across him. I tried to pull her off him but for such a substantial woman there seemed to be very little to get hold of. Boss sniffed once, walked away and lay down in the shade of the barn. His business was with dead or wounded birds and animals. Human casualties were of no concern to him.

Duggie Bracken's boots appeared beside me. 'What's adae?' he asked.

'Heart attack, I think.' He pulled his ear protectors off his ears and I repeated it. 'We'd better roll her off before she crushes him flat.'

Together we laid hands on Mrs Heminson. The limp weight was almost unmanageable but we contrived to roll her off him. Her breathing was punctuated by grunts and snorts but Old Murdo did not seem to be breathing at all.

In one of my novels I would have known exactly what to do when confronted by two inert bodies, but meeting them in reality I could only think that I needed lots of help. I looked around. Wallace and Ian were approaching along the track by the rape-field, with Ronnie, burdened by the ferret-box, on their heels. I waved to them. I must have managed to convey some sense of urgency because they broke into untidy runs and arrived winded. Ronnie paused to put down the ferret-box in the shade of the jeep.

Duggie, meanwhile, had kept his head. He had rolled Old Murdo onto his face and was applying artificial respiration in a manner which, to me, looked highly skilled.

For a second time, tragedy was drawing people like flies to blood. I could hear the tractor approaching. The sound of the power-hose was cut off and Jean Mather arrived from the direction of the house. She was splashed with mud and water, and traces of dung hung about her, but at least she was to some degree medical. Duggie sat back on his heels and made room for her. She was a different person when her profession was invoked, brisk and efficient.

'He's dead,' she said after a few seconds. 'We can't do anything for him now.' She turned to Mrs Heminson and raised one of the unconscious woman's eyelids, leaving a brown smear behind. 'Fainted. Shock, I suppose. Possible slight stroke. We'd better get her indoors and out of the sun.'

Guns were carefully laid aside. Ronnie and I took an arm each, Wallace and Ian laid hands on the thick legs but, limp and heavy, she was an almost impossible load.

'There's an old door off the house in the barn,' Duggie said helpfully.

'There's the fork-lift an' a',' said Ronnie. Jean Mather tutted at him in reproof but, having already experienced the woman's dead weight, I could see some sense in the suggestion.

The tractor had stopped nearby. While Ian broke the news to Brett, Duggie fetched the door from the barn. With Ronnie's help we managed to lift and roll Mrs Heminson onto it.

Brett broke away from Ian and joined us. His face was already badly swollen and discoloration was beginning to contrast with a new pallor. Tenderly, he smoothed down his mother's skirt and then glanced once at his father without speaking. I was preparing to become one of a stretcher party, but Brett and Ronnie stooped to an end each, lifted the door without apparent effort and started towards the house. 'I'll come and see to her,' said Miss Mather. 'And you'll need doors opened.'

Through the ironwork of the gate, the bright flowers in the garden formed a backcloth which already suggested a funeral. For want of anything more useful to do, I began to tidy up the scene. I picked up Old Murdo's stick, which was lying a few yards away, laid it neatly beside him and then gathered up the three shotguns and stowed them in the jeep.

'I'd better phone for a doctor,' Ian said. I could see the policeman in him beginning to take over. 'I just hope that he's prepared to sign the certificate.'

'I wouldn't count on any sic thing,' Duggie said. 'Yon's no heart attack. There's blood in the mannie's hair.'

We each took a step towards the body but Ian held up his hand. 'Stand where you are,' he said. He stooped and stared at the dead man's head without touching it. 'Where?'

'Abune his left lug,' Duggie said.

'It's only a spot,' Ian said. 'But there seems to be a puncture wound half hidden by the hair. Above and behind the left ear. I want everyone away from the body. Over by the barn, please.'

'He could have jabbed himself on something sharp as he fell,' Wallace said as we moved. 'Look at his stick. It has a horn handle with a sharp point.'

'He was using his stick with his right hand when I saw him,' I said. 'If the wound's on his left . . .'

Ian left us standing by the barn and went back to the body. He squatted down and looked again at the body and then at the stick. He picked up a straw and parted the thin hair. He was shaking his head as he came back.

'The wound's too deep. And I can't see any blood or hairs on the stick.' He looked at me. 'You didn't wipe it when you moved it?'

'God, no!' I said.

Ian's eyes shifted to Duggie. 'Did you see what happened?'

Duggie shook his head. 'I was diddlin' awa' at my work and I'd these on my lugs.' He lifted the ear protectors which now hung around his neck. 'I'd no idea a'thing was wrong until I saw Mr Parbitter cross the yard at the double.'

30

Ian switched his attention back to me. 'You were first on the scene, unless we count Mrs Heminson. What did you see?'

'Not much,' I said. 'I was coming across the grass field where the sheep are. I saw Old Murdo heading this way. Half a minute later his wife ran after him. They each went out of my sight. When I got round the corner, she was down beside him and trying to rouse him. Then, before I could get to them, she fainted and they were both lying as you saw them except that she was on top of him. Duggie and I managed to roll her off.'

'Right,' Ian said. He hesitated in thought.

'Could the wound have been made by a two-two bullet?' Wallace asked.

Ian looked at him sharply. 'For all I can tell at the moment. Why? Do you know something?'

'Not a damn thing,' said Wal. 'But small-bore bullets can travel a long way and still have enough energy to kill. It could have been an accident. Mr Mckee said that he'd been shooting crows. He mentioned a rifle. Well, you wouldn't use a full-bore rifle on crows, but I know that he has a two-two because I sell him his ammunition.'

'Good point,' Ian said. 'Would you fetch him for me?'

'I suppose so. Though it needn't have been him. Anybody being careless with a small-bore rifle within a mile of here could be responsible. Is it all right if I take the jeep?'

'I'll take a look at it first.'

'You won't find a rifle in it,' Wallace said. 'You know that.'

'Nor a humane killer,' I said. They looked at me in surprise. 'I don't know why I said that,' I went on, 'except that we've been hearing about a humane killer this morning and you referred to a puncture wound—'

Young Murdo came tearing along the track. Before Ian could stop him he had knelt down beside his father. He looked

31

back at us over his shoulder. 'He's dead, isn't he? What's happened to him?'

Ian took him gently by the arm, lifted him to his feet and pulled him away to where we were grouped by the barn. 'That's what we're trying to find out,' he said.

'Oh.' Young Murdo looked ready to faint. With a visible effort he pulled himself together and stooped to brush the earth off his jeans with a shaking hand. 'Does Mum know?'

'She knows,' Ian said. I suppose in a sense that it was true.

'How's she taking it?'

'Not very well. She's in the house.'

'I must go to her.' He rushed off in the direction of the house, almost colliding with Ronnie, who was returning in the opposite direction.

Ian sighed. 'Perhaps it's just as well,' he said. He saw that our eyes were being drawn unwillingly to Old Murdo's body lying in the sunshine. 'You go and fetch Ken McKee,' he told Wal.

'And if he doesn't want to come?'

'Tell him that Old Murdo's met with an accident. He'll come, if it's only to gloat. You others, go into the barn. See if you can find some stakes and binder twine. Do not go near the body or let anybody else near it until I come back. I must go and phone.'

Jean Mather had followed Ronnie. 'Mrs Heminson's shown no signs of coming round,' she said. 'She's in deep shock. I think she should be hospitalized.'

'All right,' Ian said. 'All right. I'll see to it. Now, all of you go into the barn and stay there while I use the phone in the house.' He strode off towards the farmhouse. Wallace walked to the jeep and drove off along the track by the rape-field.

'Really!' Miss Mather said. 'What a way to speak to a body!'

'He is the polis,' Duggie said apologetically. 'A whole detective inspector!'

32

In the barn we found some of the metal stakes for an electric fence and a ball of binder twine. After that, there was nothing to do but find seats and wait while, for me, Old Murdo's death changed from an event to a permanent shift in the stable local scene.

'You really think it could have been an accident?' Ronnie asked nobody in particular.

'It's hard to think it could have been anything else,' said Duggie. 'God knows, there's few enough will be sorry he's dead. But if there'd been anybody near the man, Mr Parbitter'd've seen him, or I would.'

'You don't have to be near a man to shoot him,' I said. 'But I hope you're right.'

'Mmm.' Duggie looked up at the planks from which he had been working. 'I could maybe be getting on wi' the job now.'

'Better not,' I said.

'Whit way no'?'

'Look at it from the viewpoint of the police,' I said. 'We don't know that he was shot. If anybody got at him from close to, it was his wife or you or me.'

Duggie blinked at me from his seat on a straw bale while he took in the idea. 'If it was you I'd've seen you,' he said. 'And I don't think it was me.'

'I don't think it was either of us,' I said. 'But if I were you, I wouldn't go near that nail-gun until the police have had a chance to examine it.'

Duggie started to say something, glanced at Miss Mather and checked himself. 'For Pete's sake!' he substituted.

Ronnie had seated himself on the packed earth floor. 'Just for the minute,' he said, 'we don't know if the mannie was shot or stabbed or if he landed on a spike when he fell. Half the world's troubles come from folk trying to think when they don't know what the hell they're thinking about.' He leaned back against the wall of the barn and closed his eyes.

33

Ten more minutes dragged by in silence before Ian returned. He stood against the light and looked at us. 'I may as well explain the position,' he said. 'If nothing else, it may help you to understand why you're going to be kept hanging around for some time yet. If any of you wants to phone somebody to say that you're delayed, that can be arranged.' He looked at Miss Mather.

'I used the phone while I was in the house,' she said.

'Very well.' Ian was looking harassed. 'I've made a few calls myself. My sergeant is on leave and one of my constables is off sick, so the other DC is all the skilled help I can call on in Newton Lauder.

'I've spoken to my bosses in Edinburgh. They're desperately short-handed – the Festival fetches every thief and con-man into the city. They're sending me one more DC, a forensic science technician and two SOCOs. SOCOs,' he added in explanation, 'are specially trained Scene of Crime Officers. That's all the manpower they can spare. A caravan – a mobile Incident Room – is also promised. The police surgeon should be here any minute and an ambulance is coming for Mrs Heminson. A pathologist is also on the way.

'But, for the moment, and for at least as long as the possibility of an accident remains open, it's my case. I'm to report to a detective chief inspector in Edinburgh and he'll come through when he can.

'And that's all the skilled help I can count on,' Ian said grimly. 'It may sound a lot, but it's less than half what I'll need for an unexplained death. For the rest, I'm trying to make up numbers by borrowing uniformed officers locally. The local super is going to send me out some bodies. They'll be policemen, and possibly policewomen, but they won't be trained detectives. In short, it has all the makings of a guddle. So please be patient and don't make my life any more difficult than it has to be.'

'We can hang on,' Ronnie said gruffly. He knew as well as I did that Ian's was only a token presence in Newton Lauder, his office little more than a *pied à terre* for the officers from Edinburgh who usually came to deal with any crime more serious than flashing or minor theft, giving the local man no more than a patronizing nod on the way by. Ian was being thrown off the deep end and we, his friends, would catch him if we could.

'Until skilled help arrives,' Ian said, 'does any one of you know shorthand?' He was looking at me.

'It's rusty but it still works,' I said. 'Can't your single DC do that for you?'

'He's only just been transferred from Traffic. He's only had one lesson. Until somebody more skilled turns up, you're it.'

Something else was bothering me. When I'm not writing, I get hungry. 'It's already past lunchtime,' I pointed out. 'Unless we have the run of the kitchen here, I suggest that somebody goes and explains to Alice and brings back some sandwiches.'

'You can do that,' said Ian, 'if you promise to come back. I won't need you for the next half-hour. I have some preliminary searching to do.'

'You are not searching me,' Miss Mather said loudly, but there was a hint of challenge. Ronnie stirred, apparently about to offer his services, but lost his nerve.

'Not you,' Ian said. 'Your car. And Duggie's toolbox.'

At the mention of her beloved car, a cloud passed over her face. 'I wish you joy of my car. What do you hope to find in it?'

'Your humane killer. You used it this morning?' That silenced Miss Mather. She nodded. 'And cleaned it?'

'Of course.'

'A pity.'

Miss Mather's pale blue eyes were popping. 'But surely you don't think—?'

'I can't find out what did happen without making sure what didn't.' Ian looked at me. 'One other thing before you go. Empty your pockets.'

It took me a few seconds to catch up with him. 'You think I found him alive and put a spike into his head?'

'I hope not. I want to be able to establish later that I had eliminated the possibility. After all, you did have the occasional shouting match with Old Murdo.'

'Who didn't?' I asked reasonably. Ian made no answer. I decided that he couldn't think of anybody.

I emptied my pockets onto one of Duggie's planks. Ian patted me down and made me pull up my trouser-legs so that he could see that there was no weapon tucked into my sock. 'Off you go,' he said. 'Bring back plenty. And a notebook if you have one. But don't take too long.'

I replaced a handkerchief, some coins and a couple of keys in my pockets, leaving behind several empty twelve-bore cartridge cases that I had picked up in the interests of Keeping Britain Tidy. Cattle have been known to swallow discarded cartridges, sometimes with fatal results – as Miss Mather could doubtless have confirmed. Boss came to heel without being called.

The day was, if anything, hotter and more sticky than ever. The sheep were clustering together under the beech tree that shaded a corner of the field. My legs were tired but I was glad to be out and walking again in the almost fresh air, and without the weight of rabbits cutting into my shoulder. Despite the grimness of the occasion, it was also pleasant to be able to cross the grass without expecting Old Murdo's bellow to follow me.

Tansy House stood out sharply against its backcloth of dark trees. Heading towards it, I saw an ambulance turn in at the farm road and as we reached home a car went by, driven by one of the local doctors. Black clouds were massing to the south.

36

The children rushed at me as soon as I was in at the door. I managed to convey to Alice that something untoward had happened, about which I would tell her when we had a moment's privacy, and explained that I needed the makings of lunch for six to take with me.

'I've something in the oven for you,' she said.

'No time. And this is an emergency.'

I fussed with the children for a minute and then escaped into the study, the one room that they understood to be absolutely out of bounds. When I am writing fiction on the word processor I keep note of the details of each character, as he or she develops, in a series of school exercise books. I found one of these that had been little used, crossed through the written-on pages and jotted down a synopsis of the events so far while I waited.

It took Alice only ten minutes to fill a large basket. I kissed her gratefully, because not every wife would have responded quickly and without questions to such an unusual demand, and tried the weight of it. I could lift it without great difficulty but I knew that it would weigh a ton before I could reach Easter Coullie.

As I opened the front door a police car went by. 'Bother it,' I said. I had had to learn to moderate my language as soon as Peter began to listen and repeat words. 'Half a minute earlier and I could have got a lift with them. I'd take the car, but the weather's going to break and the farm will turn into a mudbath. You'd better drop me there and bring the car back.'

Alice sighed. It would mean fetching the children away from their play and strapping them in, all for the sake of a drive of a mile or two. 'Hold on a minute,' she said. 'I think you're in luck.' And she began to wave. 'I don't mind about the food but I want the basket and things back,' she told me.

An elderly but well-kept Land Rover slowed and stopped at the foot of the steps and an elderly but less well-kept figure emerged. Sir Peter Hay, I decided, was becoming as tatty as one of his older kilts. I liked the old boy, but he did little for one's image of the well-heeled landowner.

'What's this I hear about Old Murdo being dead? Morning, my dear,' he added. He was very fond of Alice and the fact that he had reversed the sequence required by good manners was a measure of his concern.

It came back to me that Old Murdo had been Sir Peter's tenant. There was no point asking how he had heard of the tragedy so quickly. News travels with amazing speed in rural communities and Sir Peter was a natural focus for it. Ian would have phoned his Divisional HQ, the doctor and the ambulance station, and any one of those might have been enough. 'Give me a lift there and I'll tell you what little we know,' I said.

'Done,' he said. I carried the hamper carefully down the steps and we stowed it in the back of the vehicle. He looked up at Alice. 'It seems to be hello and goodbye,' he said. 'I'll come and pay my respects another time.'

'Do,' Alice said, smiling. 'Until then, hello and goodbye.'

Sir Peter kissed his hand to her. When the Land Rover was in motion, he said, 'So it's true. How is the family bearing up?'

'Shocked out of their minds,' I said.

'I wonder why. It could be a blessing in disguise.' I looked at him sharply. He caught the movement from the corner of his eye. 'Unless . . . What happened?'

'Nobody knows what happened yet,' I said. 'I wasn't far off but I didn't see anything. His wife got to him first and collapsed on top of him. This will be her now,' I added as the ambulance emerged from the farm road. 'Her sons have probably gone with her.'

Sir Peter hauled the Land Rover round into the dust left hanging by the ambulance. 'In that case I may have wasted my trip. I came to commiserate and to offer help. If he just plain went down suddenly, why all the hoo-ha and police cars rushing around? What killed him?'

'That's what we don't know. He had a head-wound, but he may have got that when he fell. Ian Fellowes is treating it as a suspicious death for the moment.'

Sir Peter was silent until he had brought the Land Rover to a halt by the corner of the barn. 'I may pay you that visit in the very near future,' he said, 'and be brought up to date.'

'You're always welcome,' I told him. 'And thanks for the lift.'

'No trouble, my boy.' He looked longingly towards the farmyard and the sad hump at the far corner of it and he sighed, torn between his love of a real-life mystery, his ready concern for his tenants and the dislike of any change which was a part of that concern. But when I had lifted the basket out of the back of the Land Rover he turned the vehicle and drove off.

THREE

At the barn, tragedy did not seem to have blunted appetites. Eyes were kept averted from the sad bundle in the yard while eager hands took the hamper from me and set it on a table that seemed to have been created by laying a door across two of Duggie's trestles. The door looked suspiciously like the one that had been used to transport Mrs Heminson but I preferred not to enquire.

During my absence, a more orderly pattern had emerged. Several cars were parked along the side of the yard furthest from the body, which still lay where we had left it. The metal stakes and binder twine had been used to fence off an area around the body and a narrow path leading to it, and a uniformed officer with a clipboard stood guard. Outside this fence, three more uniformed officers were conducting an intensive search of the conspicuously barren ground. The rabbits, which we had dropped at random, had been gathered up and hung to cool at the rear of the barn. The jeep was back near its former place and Wal was standing beside it with the sturdy figure of Ken McKee looming over him. The latter's tanned face was looking both bored and peevish.

Ian was in discussion with the doctor who, I supposed, was acting as police surgeon, but their talk finished and the doctor went back to his car. Ian came up behind the searching constables. 'Has any of you ever used a small-bore rifle?' he asked.

43

One man straightened up. 'Not often,' he said. 'But I have.'

'Then come. I suppose it's too much to hope that you can take shorthand?' The constable shook his head. Ian looked round and saw me standing in the doorway of the barn. 'You come too. You have a notebook?'

I showed him the exercise book. 'I want some lunch,' I said.

'Soon.' Ian, I could tell, was feeling the stress.

Alice had even included a tablecloth in the hamper. The others had spread it over the improvised table and were laying out her bounty on it. 'Leave some for me,' I said.

'We'll leave some,' Ronnie said. 'No' much, but some.'

Ian led us to the jeep. I opened the exercise book on the bonnet of the jeep and prepared to write.

Ken McKee must have gathered some of what was afoot, because he was noticeably defensive. 'What the hell's going on?' he demanded. 'Why have I been fetched over here and left to wait?'

'As you can see, Mr Heminson is dead,' Ian told him. 'And as you probably know, I'm Detective Inspector Fellowes.'

'You were shooting rabbits at the burn, not long back,' McKee said, as if no policeman had ever shot a rabbit.

'That doesn't alter who I am. It seems probable that Mr Heminson was shot, perhaps with a small-bore rifle. We were using shotguns. You said that you had a rifle with you this morning. Does that answer your questions?'

My eyes were down on the exercise book but in the silence that followed I could almost hear McKee wondering whether he could deny his earlier words and whether it would be politic to lose his temper. 'Are you suggesting that I shot the man?' he asked mildly at last.

Ian sighed. As my shorthand came back to me I found that I had time to consider what was being said and I supposed that any policeman must become tired of every second question being treated as an accusation. 'I don't know enough at the moment to suggest anything,' he said patiently. 'You've sense enough to see that I have to find out about every weapon being used nearby. The quickest and surest way to exonerate yourself from any possible blame is to co-operate.'

'I suppose.'

'Did you fire any shots this morning?'

'Aye. Seven or eight. At crows.'

'On the wing?'

McKee snorted. 'You'd be a better shot than me to hit a crow on the wing with a two-two rifle,' he said. 'That wife of yours could maybe do it. I wouldn't try. I put some bait out and hid myself and shot them when they landed.'

'And hung them on the fence? Or left them lying?'

'They're still where they were hit.'

'Then we shouldn't have a problem. After your argy-bargy with Mr Heminson this morning, did you fire any more shots?'

'No, I damn well didn't. I went hame to eat my dinner.'

'With your daughter?'

'She went away ahead of me.' From the tone of his voice, I was sure that McKee was hiding something.

If Ian had his own suspicions, he saved them for later. 'I want you to take this officer and show him the dead crows and where you fired each shot from. And, although it's unusual, I think that there should be an independent expert along. Wallace—'

'Now hold on a minute,' Wal said. 'I'm not an expert. I'm not even particularly good with a shotgun and I never use a rifle. Keith does all the firearms business. I deal with fishing and the business side.'

For the first time, Ian Fellowes hesitated. Like many others who come over in private life as quiet and retiring, he had an inner strength. The old Ian had now given way to the decisive police officer, but I guessed that he was feeling the strain of

45

trying to make order of a situation predisposed towards chaos. If his neatly arranged order of business was disarranged he might start making mistakes.

'Ronnie Fiddler might be more suitable,' I suggested.

For an instant, out of the corner of my eye, I thought that Ken McKee looked concerned, but Ian was pleased. Ronnie, as he knew, was a professional stalker and also spent time on vermin control. 'You're right. Thank you.' He darted over to the barn and came back with Ronnie. 'I want you to go with Mr McKee and this officer,' he said. 'Mr McKee says that he fired seven or eight shots at crows on the ground before we met him this morning, and no more after that. Mr McKee will tell the officer about his crow shooting and show him the dead birds. When you come back, confirm that what you've heard makes sense when compared with what you've seen on the ground and give me an opinion as to whether a bullet could possibly have found its way here by accident.'

'I've told you,' McKee said angrily. 'The shots were all fired before we saw Heminson alive and well and howking the vet's wee car out of the shairn.'

'If the pathologist finds a bullet in him,' Ian said, 'you may be glad that we investigated before the evidence was lost.'

'But I've no' had my dinner yet,' Ronnie said plaintively.

'Later,' Ian said.

I was childishly pleased. 'We'll save something for you,' I said. 'Maybe.'

Ronnie glared at me but he went off with McKee and the constable.

'What now?' I asked.

'Lunch,' Ian said.

Considering the inadequate warning and paucity of explanation Alice, using her considerable reserve of common sense, had done us proud. Crusty loaves, biscuits, butter, pâté, cheese, fruit and a box of mixed salad had been packed, together with all the necessary cutlery and crockery and accompanied by a variety of small cakes and pies. Assuming, correctly, that boiling water at least would be available from the farmhouse she had thrown in mugs, dried soup and teabags. The weight of the laden basket was accounted for by some cans of beer. When Miss Mather came panting back from the farmhouse with a large teapot and a kettle, a very satisfactory snack began to disappear.

Ian, I thought, would have liked to start asking questions. But a morning spent exercising in fresh air builds an appetite. He was hungry and it was clear that he could not count on the undivided attention of his witnesses or even his suspects until hunger was satisfied. He laid the foundations for an enormous sandwich and soon he was eating with as much gusto as any of us, but with his usually placid forehead creased in thought or worry.

A car eased into the yard, paused while the driver took stock and then backed up beside the two police cars. A neatly dressed man emerged. He seemed to be in no more than early middle age but he was as bald as an egg. As soon as he was clear of the car he clapped a hat onto his head.

'Pathologist,' Ian said to me. 'Dr Dunnett. I've seen him before. Come on.'

'Soon,' I said. I was as capable of procrastination as he was.

'Two minutes.' Ian hesitated and then walked to meet the pathologist, his sandwich in his hand.

In truth, I wanted to hear what he and the pathologist said to each other. I bolted my sandwich, caught them up as they followed the path to the body and prepared to write awkwardly in mid-air. The constable on duty faithfully recorded our names.

' . . . caught me at home,' the pathologist was saying, 'and I live this side of Edinburgh. I worked late last night.' He stretched and yawned.

47

'You could have taken your time,' Ian said. 'The body's been pushed and pulled around enough, but I don't want it moved more than necessary until the SOCOs are here. There's no urgency about determining the time of death – we know it to within a minute or two.'

'Understood.' Dunnett stooped over the body and moved the thin hair with the end of a spatula. 'No powder marks,' he said, straightening up. 'The cause of death would seem to be obvious, but I've been wrong before. We'll assume for the moment that we won't find poison in his stomach or a knife-wound when we turn him over.'

Ian, aware of the ears in the barn, lowered his voice. 'A bullet? Or something else?'

I had to strain my ears to hear the reply. 'I'll tell you when I open him up. From the wound, a bullet's possible.'

'Or a humane killer? Or a nail-gun?'

'Either of those, or a dozen other things. It'd have to be a big nail.'

'I've just been looking at the vet's captive bolt humane killer,' Ian said. 'It had a bolt that was thicker than a point two-two bullet.'

'You can't judge the size of a projectile from the size of the hole. The skin stretches on entry and contracts again. You'll have to be patient.'

We moved back from the body and Ian drew us away from the barn.

'At that point, is a skull thick or thin?' Ian asked.

'Thick,' Dunnett said. 'If it's a normal skull. Some are thicker than others. Again, I'll be able to tell you later.'

'But you'd expect it to be too thick to be penetrated by a spike held in the hand? Something like the icepick that keeps turning up in the movies?'

Dunnett considered. 'That would take some strength – unless the skull turns out to be thin.'

'Would you say that the wound was horizontal? Or upward or downward?'

The pathologist shrugged. 'I'd have to go back to my car for the crystal ball. From a superficial examination, the wound seems to have been made at right-angles to the skull, give or take a considerable margin. If he was standing upright at the time, which you don't know, and if he was holding his head straight, which you also don't know, it may have been more or less horizontal, which I don't know . . . yet.'

Ian scratched his neck while he thought it over. 'The track could be important,' he said, 'if we end up trying to match a weapon to the wound. Is there any way of taking a mould of it?'

Dr Dunnett smiled. 'Not that I've heard,' he said. 'A pity, really. Nice try.'

'What I think we'll do . . .' Ian paused for another moment's thought and took a large bite from his sandwich. Dr Dunnett watched him intently as Ian chewed and swallowed and he glanced at his watch. I thought that the pathologist might be making a mental note so that, if Ian were later to be found dead, he could fix the time of death by the process of digestion. 'What we'll do,' Ian resumed when his mouth was almost empty, 'is to get his head X-rayed as soon as we can move him.' He spluttered some crumbs.

'That would be best,' Dunnett agreed. 'At least you'll know whether there's a bullet in there. You appreciate that the track won't show up on X-ray?'

Ian closed his eyes for a second. It was clear that he thought that the pathologist wasn't really trying. 'You can't inject something opaque into it, on the principle of a barium enema or something?'

'Another nice try, but no. The layers of tissue and membrane are built up like your sandwich and the material would spread laterally between the layers. You'd end up with a big black blob. If we see a bullet, will the track matter so much?'

'It could,' Ian said. 'And I'm not convinced that we're going to find a bullet.'

The pathologist took a few paces to and fro while he thought about it. 'It'll be a day or two before I can get around to him, so what I'll do for you is this. I'll try to get him passed under a CT scanner. That gives you pictures representing slices through the head. It could tell you most of what you want to know about the track, although I can't hand out any guarantees. Then I'll take the first steps of an autopsy up to the point of removing the brain, recovering the bullet if there is one and if I can get at it easily, and suspending the brain in a bucket of formaldehyde.'

'For how long?'

'About ten days.' The pathologist held up a hand to quell Ian's protests. 'You either get a good result or a quick one. A brain has about the consistency of a blancmange just out of the fridge. Very difficult to section neatly and preserve the detail. Hardened by fixation in formaldehyde, I can slice it as neatly as boiled ham. And you'll have to wait a day or two for the rest of the autopsy results. He isn't at the head of the queue.'

Ian nodded unhappily. 'We'll see what the X-ray shows,' he said. He put the rest of his sandwich into his mouth.

The pathologist looked at his watch again. 'I seem to have missed my lunch. I suppose . . . ?'

'Of course,' Ian said, spitting crumbs again. 'Simon, we can spare a bite for Dr Dunnett?' he asked me.

I stopped writing. 'Be my guest,' I said. It would be poetic justice if nothing was left when Ronnie returned.

'Mr Parbitter,' Ian explained, 'is acting as my note-taker until relieved.'

Dunnett raised an eyebrow. 'Simon Parbitter, the writer?'

'That's the one,' said Ian. 'So he keeps telling me.'

50

'I've read a couple of your whodunnits,' the pathologist said. 'Call on me any time you need some gruesome advice. Would you like to attend an autopsy, some day?'

'Not a lot,' I said. 'I could force myself, in the interest of my art. But not . . . somebody I once knew.'

'I feel much the same way,' said Dunnett. 'I'm surprised how often my acquaintances turn up on the slab.'

We joined the others in the barn. The pathologist helped himself with a generous hand. Ian made another sandwich. I moved onward to coffee and a beer.

A radio had been quacking away in one of the police cars. A constable went to answer it and then came into the barn and muttered in Ian's ear. Ian, mouth full, nodded.

When they had eaten, Ian led the pathologist outside. I tagged along, exercise book in hand.

'That was a message from the hospital,' Ian said. 'The widow is recovering from shock, hysteria and the vapours. I have a constable at her bedside – alongside both her sons. She says that she was looking out of the window at her husband when he suddenly collapsed. There was nobody near him. So we can expect to find a bullet in him.'

'Unless she did it herself,' Dunnett said. 'Or unless she's protecting one of her sons. Did the farmer have a humane killer of his own?'

'I don't know,' Ian said, 'but I can find out.'

'I'll find out for you,' I said. I went into the barn and spoke to Miss Mather. I was back in a few seconds. 'He had what she called a "Point two-two Cowpuncher" but he didn't like using it himself, so if the vet was around he usually got him or her to do the deed.'

'Would Mrs Heminson have had time?' Ian asked me.

I had been pondering the same question. 'I think she would,' I said. 'But her collapse seemed to be genuine. She never twitched when Miss Mather lifted one of her eyelids.'

'Stick to firm evidence,' Ian said. 'Would it have been physically possible for her to have used the humane killer on him, returned it to the house and come galumphing out again?'

In my record I was modifying the more colloquial expressions. *Galumphing* was definitely out. 'The body's quite close to the gate to the farmhouse garden,' I said slowly. I was still finding it very awkward to speak coherently while recording my own words. 'I was some way off when I saw him vanish beyond the barn. It must have been all of a minute later when she came out of the house and went towards him at a brisk trot. I think she could have gone through the garden, in at the front door and out at the back in that time. But wouldn't Duggie Bracken have seen if she, or anybody else, had approached Old Murdo?'

'That's the first question I want to get around to asking him,' Ian said. 'More to the point, could anyone have counted on him *not* seeing them?'

The pathologist cleared his throat to attract attention. 'When I get inside his head, I should be able to tell you whether he could have walked around after his brain was penetrated. Some do, you know, even after the most extraordinary wounds.'

Ian closed his eyes for a second. 'Why are you telling me this?' he asked.

'It's not my end of the business,' said the pathologist, 'but, until I tell you otherwise, I think you should take into account that he might have been shot or spiked elsewhere and walked to where he fell. If the wife zonked him, she need never have left the house at all. Although,' Dunnett added fairly, 'I would doubt my own hypothesis if she used a humane killer. It's the speed at which the bolt penetrates the brain that gives the instant knock-down, and they're designed to be very fast indeed.'

Duggie appeared out of the barn. He was usually a jolly-looking old chap, making me think of Father Christmas without the white whiskers, but today he more resembled Grumpy in *Snow White*. 'I want to get on wi' my work,' he said peevishly.

'Not yet,' Ian said.

Duggie made a disgusted noise and turned on his heel.

'I'm rather busy myself,' said the pathologist gently.

'And I,' Ian said with great patience, 'am trying to do this by the book. The trouble is that this particular book seems to have some pages missing.' He looked up at the looming clouds. 'My one DC hasn't cast up yet and my bosses—'

At the sound of a vehicle, he stopped and waited. The same ambulance re-entered the farmyard. Ian sighed. 'My bosses are treating this as—' He stopped again and I saw relief in his face as a car that had been following the ambulance swung round to park with the others. 'This, please God, will be the SOCOs and the technician. Perhaps we can get on now.'

Three men and a young lady emerged, with the usual stretching of limbs and smoothing of clothing.

'Who's the girl?' the pathologist asked. He sounded more interested than he had while discussing such mundane matters as murder.

'We shall find out,' Ian said. Another car, this time a small and rusty saloon, ground into the yard. 'It's all happening now,' he said. 'Miracle of miracles! This is my missing DC.' He strode off to meet the newcomers.

Dr Dunnett looked at his watch. 'Bang goes most of another day,' he said to me. 'It's customary for the pathologist to show his face, but out here in the sticks a police surgeon has usually certified death long before I turn up, and there's not much I can say that he couldn't have said. If I could wait for the cadaver to arrive at the mortuary I'd get twice as much done in my life.'

'If you could call it a life,' I said.

The Scene of Crime Officers and the technician, casting their own anxious looks up at the clouds, bustled about the body. Ian returned with the two DCs in tow – his own man, a youth by the name of Strachan and barely old enough to grow a decent set of whiskers, and the girl from Edinburgh whom he introduced as WDC White. She was older than she had looked, perhaps thirtyish, very calm and competent in manner but with an attractive face and an air of sensuality which seemed to be enhanced rather than concealed by her severe dress.

'If Miss White has shorthand,' I suggested, 'perhaps you don't need me any more.'

Ian was back in his rapid thought mode. 'For the next few minutes, I want somebody to take notes at the body,' he told me, 'and that had better not be you. I want DC Strachan to take a statement from Duggie Bracken. You go with them and take it down. Sit in one of the cars.'

The young DC paled. 'But – sir—!'

'What is it now?'

'Nobody's told me anything about this case. I don't know what questions to ask.'

'That's why you need Mr Parbitter along,' Ian said. 'Between the two of them, you should know most of what you need to know by the time I want you again.' His brusqueness evaporated as he led the WDC away with an air of almost inviting her to take his arm. Deborah, I thought, had better hurry home. Ian was a vigorous young man and, in an old-fashioned force like Lothian and Borders, *droit de seigneur* might still pertain.

Young Strachan looked at me for help. 'Which is . . . whatever the name was?'

'Duggie Bracken.' I beckoned Duggie out of the barn. 'DC Strachan will take your statement,' I said. 'I'll be there to take notes. Is that acceptable?'

54

'Anything, if it lets me get on. I'm losing money,' Duggie added, as though this was the clinching argument.

We sat in the more comfortable-looking of the police cars – Strachan in the driver's seat, Duggie beside him and myself bringing up the rear. I opened the exercise book on my knee. The DC glanced anxiously over his shoulder.

'The best procedure,' I said carefully, 'would be for Mr Bracken to tell us, in his own words, what he saw and heard from before Old Murdo walked into the farmyard for the last time until he pointed out to the Inspector that there was blood in the corpse's hair.' I felt even more encumbered, taking down my own words while at the same time trying to keep the constable advised as to just what on earth we were talking about.

'Damn little,' Duggie said, 'and that's the truth. See, I was up by the beam, facing the other way, banging awa' wi' the spit-gun and wi' the muffs over my lugs. The old timmer beams was rotted and I've been putting in an RSJ. That's the steel beam,' he added helpfully. 'Last week there was enough shoring in there to hold up Edinburgh Castle. But now all I've to do is to frame the steel beam, ready to box it in.'

Around the body one of the men was taking photographs. The black clouds were almost overhead.

Duggie resumed. 'First I knew anything was adae was when you passed below me, dropping your rabbits as you went and starting to run. I looked round and there was Old Murdo down on the ground, with Bertha pulling at him. When I lifted the muffs, I could hear her screeching fit to drown a foghorn. Then she went down thump atop of him. So I slid down my ladder, canny-like, for I'm not as young as I was, and I helped you – Mr Parbitter – roll her off him. Then I took another keek at him, to see if she'd quite flattened him.

'If he was breathing it was damn little, so I turned him over – after we'd shifted her ladyship, he seemed light as a feather

– and I started the artificial respiration. I did a course once, in the First Aid. That's when I saw the blood in his hair.'

The men were sliding Old Murdo's corpse into a body-bag. I looked away. 'Let me see if I've got this straight,' I said. 'You fired shots with the nail-gun just before you saw me go by?'

'One shot, as I mind.' I noted the answer but put a large query in the margin. I would have to think back. I was almost sure that I had heard more than one shot.

'You didn't see anyone else, or anything out of the usual?' DC Strachan asked.

'Nothing.'

Strachan, still only barely aware of the morning's events, had shot his bolt. 'Could somebody have approached Old Murdo without you seeing them?' I asked.

'Aye. Easy.'

Duggie did not seem put out by being questioned by one with no proper status in the investigation so I decided to push my luck. 'Earlier today,' I said, 'before the vet turned up, you were having a row with Old Murdo. What was that about?'

'What did anyone ever argy-bargy wi' the old skin-a-louse for?' Duggie demanded rhetorically. 'Money. I was laying out the cost of materials and the mason's time for fixing the wallheid. We'd agreed I'd be paid as I went along, but when the time came did he want to pay up? Did he hell! But I got his cheque in the end.'

Here was something else that DC Strachan could get his teeth into. 'Did you indeed?' he said. 'Let's have a look at it.'

Duggie fished in a pocket of his overalls and produced a cheque filled out in a spidery hand. Looking over Strachan's shoulder, I saw that it was made out for a substantial sum.

'You see?' Duggie said. 'And now that the mannie's dead, I jalouse the cheque's no good. So I'm the last to have wanted him awa'.'

56

'The cheque never was any good,' I said. 'It's dated two years ahead.'

What Duggie said probably caused the farmer to turn in his body-bag. But Old Murdo was out of my sight in the ambulance which was already pulling out, followed by the pathologist's car. The men had pulled a plastic sheet over the ground where the body had lain. A clap of thunder drowned Duggie's next words. A moment later, the heavens opened.

'What did you say?' I had to shout the question over the drumming of rain on the roof of the car.

'Naethin' for you to scrieve.'

I closed the exercise book. I could well believe that Duggie's remark was unsuited for inclusion in a formal statement.

Somebody had left an umbrella in the car. Bumping and boring in our efforts to keep three people in the shelter of a brolly built for one, we ran to the barn where police, suspects and witnesses were sheltering together, peering out at the rain which was bouncing high off the cars and turning the farmyard to mud.

'This was all it needed to make my day,' was Ian's greeting. 'Footprints obliterated, evidence washed away. I suppose it didn't occur to any one of you three nitwits to *drive* the blasted car over here? At least it would give us somewhere private for interviews. I don't want the farmhouse disturbed yet. You.' He glared at the unfortunate Strachan. 'Bring a car over here. A roomy one, not that roller-skate of yours.'

'I'll need a key.' Strachan caught a key in mid-air, put up the umbrella again and plodded off through the mud.

'Can I get on wi' my work now?' Duggie asked.

'Later.' Ian pulled me aside and dropped his voice. 'What did you get?'

'He says that he saw and heard nothing until I ran by. I think he may be telling the truth. He thinks that he only fired one shot just beforehand but I think that I heard more than one. Make what you can of that. And he had a row with Old Murdo earlier in the day.'

57

'Over money, of course.'

'Of course. Old Murdo gave him a cheque but it was dated two years off. Duggie says that he hadn't noticed that fact until I pointed it out to him.'

Ian's eyes went out of focus for a moment as he mentally sorted out the ifs and buts. 'More complications!' he said. 'Is even Duggie so dim that he wouldn't scrutinize one of Old Murdo's cheques?'

I shrugged. 'Either way,' I said, 'it gave him a motive for wanting Old Murdo alive.'

'If he had the sense to see it.'

The car arrived and nosed half its length into the barn. 'Inside,' Ian said, singling out the detectives from the constables on loan. 'It's time for a briefing.' He supplanted Strachan in the driver's seat. WDC White got in beside him. Somehow the two SOCOs, the technician and DC Strachan managed to heap themselves into the back. We could see Ian's lips moving. The eyes of the detectives shifted from one to the other of us as he spoke. Wallace was talking to a sulky Miss Mather about the diseases of dogs and they seemed to have forgotten about the rest of us.

The jeep appeared suddenly out of the rain and stuck its nose into the barn beside the police car. The constable got out and stooped to the window of the police car. Ronnie, at the wheel of the jeep, wound his window down and I put my head inside. The interior smelt of steam, dogs and Ronnie.

'Well?' I said.

Ronnie glared at the remains of lunch. 'You didn't leave muckle.'

'I did,' I said. 'But the pathologist arrived and ate it. I didn't want to argue with him, he cuts people up. How did you get on? Could it have been an accident?'

Ronnie shrugged. 'Maybe and maybe no'. He'd put bait out and took most of his shots on the ground from a hide in a ditch. But he'd picked up his empty cases. I made him show us, and he was one short. There was another crow, outby from the others, I think the gowk had shot it out of a tree.'

'Before or after we met him?'

'No way to tell. He may've missed other high shots. In which case . . .'

'A bullet could have arrived here,' I finished for him.

'Aye. It happens. It's this way. If you shoot steeply up, the bullet comes down tumbling and wouldn't hurt a soul, no more than a wee rap on the head. Below about forty degrees, it keeps on going. And once in a million there's somebody where it comes down. There was a mannie killed on the deck of a steamer in the middle of the Clyde a few years back.'

Ronnie got out of the jeep and went over to where Miss Mather was sitting disconsolately beside Wallace on a pile of pallets. A minute or two later, I heard him trying to sell her his ancient Land Rover as a replacement for her ruined DAF.

The doors of the other car opened and the investigative team emerged. 'Right,' Ian said. He looked at Strachan. 'You follow the pathologist and catch him at the hospital. Bring back X-rays and any messages.' He switched to one of the SOCOs. 'Go with him, make sure no traces are lost from the body and then stay with it and represent me whenever the body's touched.'

'Next I want the house searched. Guns, humane killers, anything in the least out of the ordinary. There's not much else to be done until this rain lets up.' The remaining SOCO claimed the umbrella and set off towards the house followed by the borrowed constables.

That left Ian with WDC White to do his shorthand for him. 'You won't be needing me any more,' I said.

'Obviously not,' Ian said. 'You go home and type up what you've got so far.'

'Couldn't Miss White do that?'

'What shorthand do you do?' she asked.

'Pitman.'

She smiled and shook her head.

'All right,' I said. 'When I get around to it.'

'You'll get around to it straight away,' Ian said, 'unless you want your guilty secret spread around Newton Lauder.'

WDC White smirked at me. Ian ushered her into the car. Ronnie was waxing restive because Wallace had suggested that, of the two vehicles, the DAF was probably in better condition than the Land Rover. When Ian beckoned to him, he came willingly and they were soon absorbed in the business of taking his statement.

I had no intention of walking in the downpour. While I waited for a lift home in the jeep or for the rain to go off, I took a seat on one of Duggie's trestles and jotted down a bit more of my own statement.

Wallace joined me on my trestle, leaving Miss Mather to sulk on her own. 'What was that about a guilty secret?' he asked me.

I smiled.

My so-called guilty secret was that, several years before, my peripheral involvement in a rather nasty case had triggered an idea. My agent was nagging me to get back to real work after several years of writing up Keith Calder's cases under a soubriquet borrowed from a large and irritable old gentleman whom I had met, with his pair of black Ladradors, on a shoot where we were both acting as pickers-up. With considerable help from Ian on police procedures and from a psychologist friend, *Analysis of a Rape* had been born.

In this, two characters stranded in a refuge hut during a blizzard had recognized in each other the assailant and victim in a much earlier crime. The book had then flashed back to track their earlier histories, showing how each had been predisposed, he by his fear of rejection and she by her fear of

60

sin, to commit or suffer the crime. The rape itself had been recounted frankly but, I hoped, without salacity and I had gone on to describe the effect on each party of the investigation, trial and thereafter. Then, meeting again after a lapse of years, old wounds were opened, fear and guilt were exposed. During a long and emotional wait for rescue, recrimination had become compassion and the two had come to terms with themselves and each other.

Alice's reaction to reading the final draft had been to weep over the denouement and then announce that nobody must ever know who had written it. So another *nom-de-plume* had been chosen.

The book might have flared in paperback and then died the death. But it was picked up by a major and respectable publisher and, immediately after its publication, several churches, backed by the Women's Liberation Front, had demanded that it be banned. WAR (Women Against Rape) had immediately announced that it was an exact and compassionate exploration of the subject and should be made compulsory reading in schools. As a result I was interviewed, in silhouette and with my voice disguised, on three different chat shows. The book went to umpteen editions, boosted my revenue from Public Lending Rights to the permitted maximum and was still being translated into languages that I had never even heard of.

Apart from Ian himself (and, I thought, others of the Calder family who were well able to keep a secret) Newton Lauder was unaware of the authorship, although the bank manager probably had his suspicions. We were never more than slightly extravagant but it was impossible to disguise the fact that we were spending more liberally than before. It was generally assumed that we were living beyond my means, an image which was quite in keeping with the general belief that Alice and I were still unmarried. I rather enjoyed my reputation among the thrifty Borders Scots, to whom debt was an unspeakable sin.

So I smiled at Wallace and told him that it was none of his damn business.

To judge from the waving of his hands, Ronnie was attempting to explain the trajectory of bullets fired upwards at various angles. I wished WDC White joy in trying to record his explanations and turn them into a formal statement. By the time they finished, the rain was beginning to abate.

Wal joined Ian at the car. 'Do you need my statement?' he asked.

'Not urgently. I don't suppose you saw any more than I did,' Ian said, 'but you may have noticed something useful. Can you come back tomorrow?'

Wallace pretended a laugh. 'No way! The shop was closed today. Tomorrow it opens come hell or high water or Keith will want a better reason than a sudden death. And, with everyone else away, I'm the one who has to open it.'

'Go home,' Ian said after a pause. 'I'll catch up with you when I need you. I wanted Ronnie to go round the outside of the house with the SOCOs and see if he could see signs of anybody hurrying that way. Until the ground dries, we'd be doing more harm than good. From a long shot it's become an impossibility, but I'll have to go through the motions. Come back tomorrow, Ronnie. For the moment, I want to interview Miss Mather.'

'And the best of luck,' Wal said softly. 'She's about due to blow her top.'

Ian snorted. 'Well, she's not going to blow mine,' he murmured. 'Her humane killer's locked in the boot of what's left of her car. And I have the key. We haven't found Old Murdo's humane killer yet, by the way.'

'For Christ's sake,' Ronnie said, 'it's staring you in the gizz.'

He pointed at a T-shaped object hanging on the wall in a dark corner of the barn. I had taken it for a piece of plumbing or a device for turning underground stopcocks.

'That thing?' Ian said. 'We were looking for a sort of pistol.'

'It is a sort of pistol,' Wal said. 'But the operative part is shaped like one of those long torches. When you tap the end against the beast's head, that fires the cartridge and shoots the bolt in. But a bull with a hernia may not feel much like being tapped on the skull, so it comes with a long handle to wield it by. Happy now? We must go. Where's Ronnie got to now?'

Ronnie had wandered into the back of the barn and was in conference again with Miss Mather. I went to fetch him. 'The engine's a'most new,' he was saying.

'It's not the engine I'd be worried about,' said the vet, 'it's the rest of it. I might know a farmer who'd buy it for the sake of the engine.'

'Who?'

'If I find you a buyer,' Miss Mather said, 'will you fill up my insurance claim form for me? Please?'

I decided that the vet was not as silly as she seemed. Explaining, within the confines of an insurance claim, how her car had managed to drive itself into a tank of dung and then be wrecked by the possibly well-intentioned actions of a man now deceased was a task that was not to be entered into lightly. Ronnie evidently agreed with me. He turned away without a word.

We piled into Keith's jeep. At the road-end we met a large caravan towed by a police Range Rover. Two minutes later Wallace pulled up outside Tansy House.

'Coming in?' I asked.

Ronnie and Wal raised eyebrows at each other.

We ran up the steps through the last of the raindrops. Pandemonium arrived as we were wiping our feet in the hall.

63

As Alice came out of the kitchen, Peter hurled himself at me, shrieking with pleasure, while Jane toddled after to grab at the basket which now held my share of the rabbits. I put down the basket of rabbits and hefted both children up, one under each arm.

Alice was visibly alight with curiosity but, as always, her instinct as a hostess came first to the fore. 'Hullo,' she said. 'You must all be hungry.'

'Just starving. These bug... burgh... beggars,' Ronnie said, glancing at the two children, 'ate it a'. Didn't leave me a bite.'

'Can you both stay for a meal?'

'Is there any food left in the house, after the lunch you provided?' I asked her.

'Ample. I shopped yesterday.'

'I'd be glad,' Ronnie said. He lived alone.

'Janet's away until tomorrow night,' Wal said. 'I'd only be having a bar snack at the hotel. If you're sure?'

'Quite sure,' Alice said. 'Just keep these two out of my hair for a while. Who's going to tell me what on earth's going on?'

'Not while little ears are listening,' I said. 'We'll fill you in later.'

What I liked to think of as the Age of Affluence had made little difference to the comfortably plain sitting room except for a new carpet and curtains and some fresh upholstery to my uncle's old chairs. Ron and Wal settled and I dropped a child onto each of their laps.

My offer of drinks was accepted. Since the dawning of the Age of Affluence, my drinks cupboard was a great deal better stocked than ever before. In particular, I could indulge a taste for the better malt whiskies. I poured three of these plus an extra beer for Ronnie and orange juice for the children.

Ronnie put Jane on the floor and got up to collect his drinks

– but not out of eagerness, I was surprised to note. He took the two glasses from me but put them down again on the mantelpiece, out of reach of small hands, and glowered at the large-scale map that I had hung on the wall. A frown of deep thought sat uncomfortably on his beetling brow.

'Will you two keep an eye on the kids?' I asked. 'I'd better go and start typing up Ian's statements for him.'

'Bide a wee,' Ronnie said. 'How far was . . . it . . . moved, afore I saw it?' he asked suddenly.

'I think it was still within a yard of where it fell,' I said. 'Duggie rolled it over once to start his artificial respiration.'

'Then I doubt if Ken McKee's to blame for an accident.' Ronnie planted a large finger on the map. 'Here's where I think he took his air-shot from, but even if he'd moved to the furthest corner of his own land—' Ronnie picked up a book and used the spine as a straight edge. 'Aye. I thought as much. From there to where . . . it . . . was lying, the corner of the barn would have been in the road.'

'You're sure?'

'No. I'll have a look, the morn.' He sat down and took Jane back on his knee.

'Keep each other company for a minute,' I said.

I carried my drink through to the study. I only intended to make a token start to Ian's typing, to have something to show in case of a sudden enquiry as to how I was getting on. But, as always when words began to make patterns on the screen of the word processor, time lost all meaning. It seemed only a few seconds later when Alice called me through and I realized that I was left with only Duggie Bracken's statement to finish. My drink was untouched.

The scene in the sitting room was much as I had left it. Peter and Wallace were using Lego to create a structure vaguely resembling Edinburgh Castle. Ronnie was helping Jane with an educational puzzle involving the placing of shaped blocks

65

in matching holes. He seemed to be making heavier weather of it than she was, but I hoped that he was only pretending. The children, I saw, were already bathed and in pyjamas.

'We eat in twenty minutes,' Alice said. 'You can take them up to bed and tell them their story.'

'Can we come and listen?' Wallace asked.

'Certainly not,' I said. 'It'll be much too intellectual for you. Stay down here and tell Alice what's been happening. Help yourselves,' I added unnecessarily.

I gathered Jane up. Peter, as usual, took hold of my trouser pocket and we climbed the stairs. It was the one moment of any day when I felt truly paternal.

As the professional story-teller of the family, this duty usually fell to me. But it was never easy to pitch it at a level that Jane, only just three, could understand and yet interest Peter who was either six or seven. However, I embarked once more on the saga of two children who continued to outwit a wicked ogre who sometimes took on a remarkable resemblance to Ronnie, keeping it simple until Jane fell asleep and then building to a gentle climax. Each had inherited Alice's dark copper hair and their heads glowed in the lamplight. When Peter's grip on my sleeve relaxed, I kissed them both and tiptoed out of the room.

FOUR

The uncle from whom I had inherited Tansy House had used the former dining room as a study and Alice, although occasionally regretting the lack of a separate dining room, had insisted that I continue the arrangement. We were taking our places at the table that occupies the dining end of the sitting room when the front doorbell chimed. Alice darted to it before I could get up and came back with Ian Fellowes. He looked drawn.

'Another grass widower,' she said. 'Sit down with us, Ian. The food will stretch. Do you want to wash first?'

'He can't break bread with his suspects,' I said.

Ian glanced at the table, sniffed the savoury smells and swallowed. I guessed that he had been sustained by no more than the sandwiches and coffee that are the usual portion of police in the field. 'I could break suspects with my bread,' he said. 'Not that I think any of you qualify as suspects. Ronnie and Wal have an excellent alibi – me – and you, Simon, weren't out of my sight for more than a few seconds. I'll wash.'

He was back in a minute, looking better but still the policeman rather than the sociable Ian, and took the extra place that Alice had set. I offered him a drink but he shook his head. 'I shan't count myself off duty until this is over,' he said. 'Have you done that typing for me?'

'Nearly finished,' I said.

'Can I see it?'

'It's still on disk. You can read it off the screen if you like, or I'll finish and print it and bring it to you in the morning.'

To have opened a bottle of wine would have seemed like a celebration of death. But whisky was a proper drink for a wake and beer was permissible. The mind generates its own etiquette at times of disaster. I brought beer to the table while Alice served the meat. The evening light was beginning to fade. I switched on the lamps. When I went to draw the curtains I saw that more lights than usual were showing at Easter Coullie Farm and I shivered.

'You know what's happened?' Ian said to Alice.

'Most of it, I think. Wallace told me what he knew while Simon was typing.'

Ian looked faintly distressed. Any detective would vote for a law that forbade the public from speaking to one another. He filled his mouth and chewed, making little mewing sounds of pleasure, following it with a sip of water. 'The whole case has turned on its head again,' he said. 'The one thing I can say for sure is that Ken McKee didn't kill Old Murdo accidentally by letting off a shot at a crow.'

'Ronnie was just working that out,' I said. 'The corner of the barn would have been in the way.'

'Right.' We waited while Ian filled his mouth again. 'The pathologist came back in person,' he said at last, 'to give me the result of the X-rays. I don't know that you're going to believe this. I'm not sure that I believe it myself.'

'Believe what?' Wallace asked.

'So I'm glad I caught you here,' Ian said. 'With Keith away, I've no other source of quick and specialized advice.' He filled his mouth and started chewing again while looking thoughtfully at the water jug.

I decided that Ian had not set out to tantalize but simply was unaware that we did not yet know what he was talking about. There was one quick way to bring him back to the real world. 'Have your ferrets had a meal?' I asked Ronnie.

He caught on immediately. 'Aye. Alice gied me a dishie and some milk and bread. That'll do them for now.'

Ian returned to the present. 'The X-rays,' he said. 'They show a flattened metallic pellet that had passed most of the way through the brain. It is obviously too small to be a conventional two-two bullet. His opinion, and mine, is that it's an airgun slug. Impossible to say, until he gets it out, whether it has rifling marks – if, indeed, any marks survive the damage.'

'Wow!' I said. That did indeed turn the case on its head. We waited for Ian to go on, but he had filled his mouth again. 'Didn't the pathologist say that it had passed through a thick part of the skull?' I asked.

Ian nodded.

'Was his skull thin, then?' Ronnie asked.

Simultaneously, Ian shook his head and shrugged. I interpreted the combination to mean that the pathologist had given him no more than a preliminary opinion.

'Well, I don't get it,' Wal said. 'The common air rifle is restricted by law to an energy level – twelve foot-pounds, I think – which is reckoned to be safe. A lead slug wouldn't penetrate a normal skull.'

Ian had recovered the power of speech. 'That's why I stopped here when I saw the jeep outside. I need your help. You' – he looked at Ronnie – 'are a stalker with experience of a wide range of firearms. You' – he switched to me – 'have been writing up all of my father-in-law's cases, so you must have picked up at least some smattering of the subject. And you, Wallace, are a partner in a gunshop. Yes,' he added quickly as Wallace began to object, 'I know. You're the fishing and business partner. But you often deal with airguns. Right?'

71

'I sell them,' Wal admitted. 'Sometimes I work on them, to the extent of replacing springs and washers. But Keith's the expert.'

'All the same, give me an opinion. How difficult a job is it to fit a more powerful spring?'

'Given basic tools, heat and a little knowledge,' Wal said, 'any fool can make a spring. I've done it myself. But to make a new mainspring for a particular airgun, that's a different matter. A coil spring gets fatter as it's compressed. Also, a heavier gauge spring won't compress as far, because the wire's thicker. It would be easy to get it wrong.'

'It's a job for a gunsmith?'

Wallace looked thoughtful. 'Or at least for a competent mechanic who's a bit of a mathematician. And the common airgun wouldn't stand up for long to the extra loading.'

'Do you know,' Ian asked bluntly, 'whether Keith has ever done such an alteration?'

Wallace's eyebrows went up. 'Ever's a long time. You'd have to ask him. As far as I know, he's never done such a thing since I've known him, and that's been a matter of twenty years or more. It wouldn't always have been illegal,' Wal pointed out.

Ian thought that over and then looked at me. 'You saw and heard Young Murdo using his air rifle. Did it sound normal?'

'It sounded exactly like any other air rifle,' I said. 'It just went *Phut!*. Of course, I was comparing it with the much louder banging of twelve-bore shotguns. But you surely can't suspect Young Murdo. He's a gentle soul.'

Ian looked at me without comment.

'Even a gentle soul has a limit,' Ronnie said. 'You saw how his dad treated him. And then to forbid him seeing his lady-love. I thought at the time that he was maybe pushing the boy too far. A' the same, unless your pathologist mannie finds a thin skull, it's just not possible. For a big enough bet, I'd stand

72

sideways and let you ping me on the heid wi' a slug out of that gun at twenty yards.' He waited expectantly but in vain for offers.

'I'll have to get my hands on that air rifle,' Ian said. 'Young Murdo's still at the hospital with his mother but I had somebody ask him the question. He says that he just dropped it and ran when he saw that something was wrong at the farmhouse. We haven't found it yet.'

'If you want a keek at it,' Ronnie said, 'I've got it in the back of the jeep. When we went wi' Ken McKee, I spotted it lying beside the track where he'd dropped it, along with his bag of bits. There was rain coming and you don't leave a good gun, or even a cheap air rifle, lying in the wet grass. And his Cymag shouldn't get wet at all. It was in a tin, but tins can leak and it's the damp in the ground that releases the cyanide gas when you spoon the powder down a hole. I'll show you the gun later.'

'Fetch it now,' Ian said. He remembered his manners. 'I'm sorry, Alice. I shouldn't be bossing people around in your house.'

'Carry on,' Alice said. 'You're an object lesson. I'm still hoping to get the knack of it.' She winked at me.

Ian was still too tense to laugh but at least he smiled for a moment. 'I can't imagine there being any useful fingerprints on it,' he said, 'but whenever I take a short cut it turns out to have been a wrong turning. Alice, do you have a large, clean polythene bag?'

Alice nodded. 'A pair of Simon's trousers just came back from the cleaners. They're still in the bag. Where are they, Simon?'

'I hung them behind the study door,' I said, 'just to have them out of the way.'

'Use that,' Ian told Ronnie. 'I won't even come out with you. Your fingerprints will be all over it anyway. We'll take

73

your prints for comparison purposes when you come over in the morning.'

Ronnie had cleared his plate but he grumbled as he got up from the table. He returned with the airgun in the thin polythene.

'This is it?' Ian asked me.

'It looks much like it,' I said.

Ian took it from Ronnie and gave it to Wal. 'What do you think? Try to handle it by the extremities.'

It was a conventional barrel-lever action. Wal put it over his knee and broke it open, checked that there was no slug in the barrel and felt the strength of the spring. Working awkwardly through the polythene bag, his movements were slightly clumsy. Some tasks were made more difficult by the absence of three fingers from his right hand.

'It feels absolutely normal,' he said. 'I can test it in the morning if you want.'

'I'll have it printed and sent over to you. And there was another air rifle in the house. I'll have it fetched to you for testing.' Ian carried the gun out into the hall and I heard him deposit it in the umbrella stand. When he resumed his seat he looked at Wallace again. 'We'll stay with you for the moment,' he said. 'You know what happened. Old Murdo fell down dead with a . . . a projectile in his brain which shouldn't have been able to penetrate his skull. What explanations can you envisage?'

Wal looked thoughtful. 'Apart from a souped-up but otherwise ordinary airgun? There are two other ways.'

I had got up to help Alice clear the dishes and serve a sweet course but I was still paying attention. 'Three,' I said.

'We'll come back to you in a minute,' said Ian. 'The mystery writer's mind might throw up something feasible for once. Go on, Wal.'

Ever the meticulous accountant, Wallace wanted to define

his parameters. 'Do you want a purely technical answer, ignoring questions such as who, from where, with what and why?'

'Those questions are for me to answer,' Ian said. 'Lucky me!'

'Very well, then. Firstly, high-powered air rifles are made. They require a firearms certificate. They aren't regularly imported into this country but they can be ordered specially. We've sold one or two from the shop and you can trace them from the records. I remember a Crossman Model 140 going through the shop but I don't remember who bought it. There may very easily be others held illegally. If somebody decides to bring one back in his luggage from a trip to the States, the Yanks don't give a damn. At this end, he could walk through the green lane with it and if somebody took a look in his luggage I have my doubts as to whether customs'd think twice about it.

'And, secondly, you've got the antiques.'

Ian's eyebrows shot up. 'This is the first time I've heard of an antique airgun.'

'Well, it would be,' Wal said. 'You wouldn't have come across them when you were acting as Firearms Officer, because a genuine antique isn't subject to the Firearms Act. A collector would only have to register it if he wanted to fire it. That would turn it from a museum piece back into a firearm.'

'But . . .' said Ian. He came to a halt.

Alice decided to finish the question for him. 'Could an antique airgun kill somebody? I thought that airguns were modern toys.'

'Neither modern nor toys,' Wal said. 'Most of the earlier ones were bored for a ball larger than two-two, but a barrel liner wouldn't be much of an engineering feat to make. Later, they came in Number Two bore, which is our modern two-two. Once again, Keith's the expert; but we had an air cane

75

through the shop last year and Keith read me a lecture. Airguns certainly go back to the sixteenth century and possibly much earlier. Which is what you'd expect when you remember that an air weapon could be loaded today and fired next week, unlike the matchlock; and, what's more, an air weapon could be fired in the rain. Even the best flintlock, when eventually it arrived on the scene, was unreliable in the wet. The so-called "waterproof" flashpan usually ended up full of sludge. You're into the nineteenth century before you have a firearm you could rely on in the rain.

'By the mid-eighteenth century, some very efficient pump-up repeating airguns were being made. In seventeen-eighty the Austrian army adopted the Girardoni. It was accurate up to a hundred and fifty yards, which is more than you could say for some of the contemporary muskets, and with no smoke and little sound it was a valuable weapon of surprise. It was only withdrawn in eighteen-fifteen because of servicing problems.'

'You sound more like Keith every day,' Ian said grumpily. 'Come to the point. Nobody wants a lecture.'

'I do,' I said. 'But I'll get it out of Keith some other time.'

'Well, all right,' Wallace said. 'The point is not to think of them as toys. Some of the best known London makers built them.

'Then, in the nineteenth century, came the "walking stick" airgun or "air cane". You already had walking sticks with swords and daggers hidden in them. Others were disguised shotguns. The pump-up air cane looked clumsy for a walking stick, but it was very powerful as a weapon.'

'So I could be looking for a collector?' Ian suggested.

'Perhaps, but not necessarily. They were very popular with poachers, keepers and lairds. Two for the weight of one. Some farmer could still be using his grandfather's air cane, quite unaware that it ought to be on his Firearms Certificate.'

Wallace paused dramatically. 'I rather think that Ken McKee may have been leaning on one when we met him yesterday.'

A stillness settled on the table. Alice froze in the act of pouring coffee. 'Oh please,' she said, 'no. Not the McKees. I like them. They're the best neighbours anyone could have.'

'True as that is,' I said, 'it doesn't exonerate them. Old Murdo's name was a dirty word in the McKee household.'

'Yes it does,' Alice said. 'Exonerate them, I mean. They just wouldn't.'

Ian was trying to hide his sudden interest. 'I'll check into it as soon as I leave here,' he said. 'Meantime,' he looked at me, 'you suggested another possibility.'

'Was there a two-two rimfire rifle in the house?' I asked.

'There was. And not properly secured,' Ian said grimly. 'In fact, it was standing loose behind the back door. Exactly the sort of carelessness the Firearms Act was designed to stop. I'd have had a word about that with Old Murdo if he'd still been around. As it is, I suppose the family will let him take the blame for any infringements of the Act.'

'And were there any blanks for a dummy launcher or humane killer?'

'There were blanks for a humane killer,' Ian said. 'But the humane killer in the barn doesn't seem to have been used for years.'

'That may not matter,' I said. 'The humane killer could have drifted into disuse if Old Murdo preferred to leave killing to the vet, but the blanks were still around. Somebody may have wanted to kill Old Murdo in such a way that somebody else would be blamed. If he shoved an airgun pellet into the breech of a small-bore rifle with a blank up its backside, wouldn't that do the trick?'

'Aye, likely,' Ronnie said. 'But I have my doubts.' He paused, swallowed and looked around bashfully while choosing his words. 'Here's how I see it,' he said. 'You take a proper, full-bore rifle. You hit a deer with it, or a man, and the bullet arrives with a mighty wallop. It flattens, or breaks up. Shock and speed are the killers as much as the damage.

'A two-two, now, that's different. More like a thin stab-wound. To kill, it's to be in just the right place.

'But a waisted airgun slug . . . Never heed the velocity, it's meant to be accurate over a short distance. It'd soon lose speed, let alone accuracy, over more of a range. He'd've had to be shot from the barn or a corner of the house, not much further than that.'

'Even by a skilled marksman?' Ian asked.

'How good is good?' Ronnie retorted. 'What I'm saying is that I don't believe you'd get accuracy, using a pellet in front of a blank. It might have the power, I wouldn't know. But even then you couldn't be sure of killing. Folk have walked and talked and lived after major head-wounds.'

'Quite true,' Ian said. 'The pathologist was telling me of a man who took the blast of a shotgun through the back of his head. Most of the shot came out through his right eye. He shoots off the left shoulder, now, Dunnett said, but otherwise you wouldn't know.'

Alice had been listening in rapt silence. Now she moved and cleared her throat, turning gently pink when she had caught our attention. She was always shy when expounding an original thought to an audience of more than one or two. 'I was thinking much the same as Ronnie,' she said. 'And I wondered. Does anybody have an airgun pellet?'

Ronnie fished in his pocket. He found several airgun pellets among a few .22 cartridges (both spent and fresh), a pocket knife, a box of matches and several gaudy fishing flies embedded in a cork.

'And a toothpick?' Alice asked.

From among his treasures, Ronnie produced a toothpick. The wood looked dark grey, almost black. 'It's been used,' he said, 'but if I gie'd it a wee whittle . . .'

Alice's nostrils widened. 'I am not going to clean my teeth with a second-hand toothpick, thank you very much. And I'm trying very hard not to think about who would have had to do this if anybody did it.'

'Quite right,' Ian said. 'That's my job.'

'All right, then. Just suppose,' Alice said, 'that somebody stabs him in the head with a humane killer or a nail-gun, or just something spiky like a bradawl or an icepick or even just a nail and a hammer. He walks off, dazed but still alive, and collapses in the yard. They run after him.'

'An airgun slug has a hole in the back going a long way into it.'

'That's so that air pressure will expand the skirt against the rifling,' Wallace said.

'Never mind why. The point is that it does.' Alice broke the toothpick and pushed it into the pellet. 'A thin pencil would do it, or a piece of wire. Somebody could have pushed a used airgun pellet into the hole and been out of the way before Simon came round the corner of the barn.'

'You realize,' Wallace said severely, 'that you're pointing a finger at the widow?'

'I'm not pointing at anybody,' Alice said. 'As Ian already told us, that's his job. I'm just suggesting one way it might have happened.'

Ian took the scrap of wood from her, with the airgun pellet clinging to the end like the head of a drumstick. 'Well done,' he said. 'Up to now, I've been doing more gathering of information than theorizing, but I had been starting to wonder, rather vaguely, whether there wasn't an alternative to the McKees and an antique air cane. But there are snags. Do you have a blancmange handy?'

Alice made a pocket-patting gesture and shook her head. 'What on earth do you want a blancmange for? There's a jelly in the fridge if that's any good.'

'I don't know that I do want one, particularly. But the

pathologist likened the texture of the brain to a blancmange just out of the refrigerator. If you'd had one, I was considering spiking a hole in it and then inviting one of you to try to insert that slug in a way that wouldn't leave the sort of traces that could be detected at autopsy. I'd expect to see a double track, matter pushed ahead of the slug or the slug not pushed as far as the spike had penetrated, something like that.'

'The jelly'd be better than the blancmange,' Ronnie said earnestly. 'You could see what was happening inside. Let's do it. We could shoot a slug in, for purposes of comp . . . comparison.' The bottle had, by then, gone round rather often.

'The jelly would probably burst all over the room,' Alice said.

'We'll go into the garden.'

'No.' Alice sounded as though she meant it. Ronnie subsided unhappily. For some reason, he was finding the idea of shooting airgun pellets into a jelly attractive.

'Anyway, it would probably behave quite differently when not confined in a skull,' Ian said. 'What makes it all the more difficult is that, to judge from the X-rays, the slug is more than a little flattened. It doesn't look as if there will even be enough rifling marks left to be of any help. So I doubt if there's much of a hole left in the back of it for pushing a stick into. And the scenario, as Alice has outlined it, suggests that somebody was very quick witted and took advantage of an unexpected opportunity to cover up their own crime – or somebody else's, did you think of that? It would be a miracle if they just happened to have a used and flattened airgun slug handy.'

It seemed to me that he was leaping too far ahead. 'Unless it was all premeditated. Suppose that the culprit had planned to insert the slug when he fell down at their feet,' I suggested. 'The fact that he managed to walk a few yards would only demand a modification of the original plan.'

'Again, quite true,' Ian said. I had the impression that we had been covering ground over which he had already travelled in his mind but that he was glad to see his thinking given a public airing. 'We may know more after the autopsy.'

'Or possibly not,' I said. 'Unless you want to wait ten days. Your pathologist sounded pessimistic.'

'The brain being like a blancmange, and so forth,' Alice said helpfully.

Ian helped himself to biscuits and cheese. 'You heard what the pathologist told me, Simon,' Ian said. 'You explain.'

'He said that the track of the bullet will have gone through layers of tissue and brain that are built up like a sandwich. If, for instance, he injected into the track some liquid that was opaque to X-rays, it would leak out between the layers with the result that the X-rays would show a large blob and no information. I thought he was going to arrange for a CT scan,' I added.

Ian pushed his plate away and looked at his watch. 'He was going to try. With a little luck, they're doing it now. He went into more detail later and he didn't promise too much. It seems that a bullet interferes with the X-ray beams so that, unless the exposure's carefully adjusted, the bullet appears like a starburst and the track is obscured. In a negative sort of way it's like trying to take a photograph of something near the sun.

'I said that if he could get some good pictures of the track, clear enough to show whether the slug was pushed into an already prepared hole, he could go ahead and dangle the brain in formaldehyde. That way, the very best evidence can be preserved. If he can get the slug out without damaging the track, he'll do it. Otherwise we won't know what evidence it can provide for some days.'

'That seems to be the best you can do,' Wallace said. 'Simon, do you think that Duggie could have—'

'At this point,' Ian said, 'I must draw the line. You're intelligent enough people to figure out for yourselves who the suspects would have to be, but it would be quite wrong of me to discuss police theories with private citizens. You can go ahead and speculate endlessly with your mates about who did what and how, but you're not going to be able to say "Ian Fellowes suspects so-and-so." I don't want to sound toffee-nosed, but that's the way it is. I don't think there can be any objection to seeking your expert opinions about methods.

'Which reminds me – Wal, are you expecting Keith to phone?'

'With Keith,' Wallace said, 'who knows?'

'If you get a call from him, get him back here, soonest.'

'He won't come if he's enjoying himself.'

'And he'll be enjoying himself,' Ronnie said.

'He'll come,' Ian said. For the first time since Old Murdo's death he produced his familiar grin. 'If he calls, tell him that a beautiful blonde is being falsely accused of murdering her faithless lover with an antique dagger.' He paused, frowning. 'No, not a dagger. Too commonplace. Make it a Doune pistol. That should fetch him back,' he added with satisfaction. 'If Deborah phones, I'll get her to pass on the same message.'

'It has all the elements,' Alice said. She giggled suddenly. 'If the car isn't fast enough, he'll get out and run.'

'That is the general idea. And now I must run along and pay a call on Ken McKee. After that I suppose I'll have to advise Edinburgh that an accident seems to have been very unlikely.' He raised his hands and let them fall. 'My first big solo case and every obvious solution is just as obviously fit to be laughed out of court. I don't know whether I'll be glad or sorry when somebody more senior takes over, but at least they'll have the clout to get more back-up.

'Ronnie, I want you to come back to the farm in the morning. It's a slim chance after all the rain, but you may be able to spot some track that my men would miss. I've spoken to Sir Peter and he agrees.

'Wal, look out the shop's records, please. Antique or powerful air weapons; and I'd like a list of purchasers of two-two pellets, insofar as you and Janet can remember them.

'Simon—'

'I'll finish the typing and bring it to you in the morning,' I said.

'I had hoped,' Ian said, 'that that went without saying. The WDC they sent me can cope from here on, but they could only spare her an old sit-up-and-beg typewriter. Could she have some time on your word processor, please?'

'She can't take it away,' I said. 'She's welcome to come and use it here.'

'That'll do,' Ian said. 'And Alice—'

'Yes?' she said brightly. 'You have a job for me?'

Ian got to his feet and smiled. 'Don't tempt me while I'm desperately short of manpower. I was only going to thank you for the meal. And thank you all. You've been very helpful. And one more thing . . . Wal and Ronnie, you'll neither of you be fit to drive by the time you've exhausted the Parbitters' hospitality, so take a taxi or get Alice to run you home.'

With Ian's steadying influence removed, a jolly party developed over the washing up and only one plate was broken. We settled in the sitting room with more coffee and drinks. Silence descended over us like a restive mother hen. We had been laughing as an antidote to emotional conflict.

Talk, when it resumed, was at first about the day's rabbiting, Alice's dinner, almost anything except the death of Old Murdo. It had been too much in our minds and the fact that he had been inviting everybody's enmity for years somehow made it worse, as if it was impossible to mention him at all without speaking ill of the dead. From time to time, somebody would feel the need to say something good of the dead man, in qualified remarks such as, 'He was a good father to the boys – when he was younger' and 'He never neglected his beasts – when he remembered'. I thought that I would rather be totally forgotten than remembered without affection or respect.

But, inevitably, our minds were teasing at the puzzle and it only took a word from Ronnie to set us going. 'You had the right of it,' he said suddenly, looking at me. 'Old Murdo was shot. And if he was shot wi' a two-two airgun pellet it most likely was the way you said.'

'You could be right,' Wallace said. 'But why? Pass the bottle.'

Ronnie passed the bottle and cogitated. I was coming to realize that he was quite capable of rational thought but was not used to verbalizing it. On the other hand, drink had loosened his tongue. 'Take 'em yin at a time,' he said at last. 'Miss Mather could have used the humane killer, the wee captive bolt one – the thirty-two pistol's for horses and cattle. She's a jolly woman, mostly, but she was mad as a cat that's lost its kittens over the damage to her car. It was only insured third-party and there was no need for the old devil to wreck it as he did. What's more, she's still on appro—'

'In her probationary period, you mean,' I put in.

'Aye, just that. If Old Murdo had got her in shit with her boss, the partnership might never have been confirmed.'

'Her boss knew Old Murdo's charming ways,' I said. 'I've seen the pair of them in a slanging match before now.'

'She mightn't have known that he knew it,' Ronnie pointed out. 'Or then there's Duggie wi' his nail-gun. They make nails up to four inches for it, I've seen them used. He might've looked at the cheque and seen he'd been diddled. For a' we ken, either of them could've had time to follow him up and stick in a pellet.'

'Duggie's getting stiff,' Wallace said. 'Too stiff to hurry up and down ladders. Simon, did you see him up on the beam?'

'Of course not,' I said. 'I was looking at what seemed to be two corpses laid out in the farmyard. I'd heard him using his nail-gun, though.'

Wallace raised his eyebrows. 'But was he using it on Old Murdo? Or did you hear Jean Mather using the humane killer on him?'

I shrugged.

'Was the spray moving around?' Wal persisted. 'Or could it have come from a fixed hose?'

'I think it was moving,' I said. 'But if the hose had been fixed a foot or two from the end it could waggle around.'

Ronnie seized the initiative again. 'But Bertha Heminson says she saw Old Murdo collapse and then she came running out. So if Duggie or Jean Mather did it, Bertha'd have to be covering up for them. And why would she do that? Do you think she wanted to be free to become Mrs Bracken?' Ronnie paused and gave a little shudder at the thought of such a coupling.

'Bertha could ha' done it herself. But why would she? She's the only one who cares that he's gone. The two of them might have their differences, whiles, but at any kind of real trouble they'd close ranks. And – by God! – you daren't say a word against Old Murdo where she could hear you.

'If one of the boys had killed his father, she'd cover up for him a' right. Old Murdo was right coarse to the both of them and he wouldn't hear of it when Brett wanted to go to the Agricultural College. But why would they bother wi' spikes and a bullet on a stick? Young Murdo was down our way and only an ordinary airgun wi' him, but where was Brett? I'll tell you,' Ronnie added quickly rather than allow one of us to usurp the conversation while he was in a mood of rare garrulity. 'He was round and about on the tractor. I asked him.

85

He moved some sheep, patched some fences and did a dozen other wee tasks, and in between he fetched the dead ewe back o'er the brig. If he came back to the farmhouse, who'd notice – except maybe his mum? He could have taken the two-two rifle, put a pellet up the spout and a blank behind it and shot his father from the garden gate. At that short range, the pellet would hold straight enough. The rifle could've been cleaned and back in its place in time for Brett to arrive on the tractor when he did.'

Ronnie fell silent while he gave his full attention to refilling his glass. We were well on the way through a second bottle by then.

'You make a good case against Brett,' Wallace said. 'Maybe you've missed your vocation, Ronnie. You should have been an advocate.'

'I'd ha' looked fine in a wig and gown,' Ronnie said.

'But why would Brett use an airgun pellet? If it was to divert attention from himself it was hardly logical. There was another airgun in the house.'

'The other one's smaller calibre,' I said. 'A one-seven-seven. I've seen the boys out with them. And it's quite possible that he couldn't get at the two-two rifle cartridges. Old Murdo reserved to himself the right to use the rifle. He said that it was because he couldn't trust either of them to use it safely, but I think he was just being thrawn.'

'But Brett wouldn't try to divert suspicion onto his own brother,' Alice said. She sounded scandalized.

'Aye, he would,' Ronnie said. 'They're close, those two, but they were aye driven to blaming each other when Old Murdo went on the rampage about some wee misdeed around the farm. Likely it got to be a habit.'

The others were nodding, convincing themselves that Brett was a patricide.

'Anyway, Brett wouldn't have to do complicated things with

airgun pellets,' Alice said. 'He could have had an accident with the tractor and nobody could ever have proved that it was done on purpose.'

'There's another good suspect,' I pointed out. 'Ken McKee. I know he's a good neighbour, but he was always at odds with Old Murdo, and since Young Murdo started courting the McKee girl they've been at each other's throats. To cap it all, calling young Sheila a whore. Many men have been killed for less.'

'But how?' Wallace asked. 'Ken McKee has a stiff leg. I can't see him crawling through the rape.'

'Very simply. His land abuts on Easter Coullie right round almost to where we started rabbiting this morning. Ken McKee decided to have it out with Old Murdo, so he crossed the boundary and walked down the main farm track. He wasn't hiding himself, he didn't have murder in his mind at the time. But we were down in the gully until I headed off round the other side of the farm buildings and Mrs Heminson was inside the house. Nobody need have seen him, except perhaps Brett if he wasn't concentrating on his fences at the time.

'Either he met Old Murdo and they had another blazing row, or else he just boiled over when he saw the old sinner. He was walking, with his air cane already loaded in case he got the chance of a crow, and he used it from about the corner of the barn. All he had to do after that was to duck in among the farm buildings. A minute or two later we were all concentrating on the body and he could have gone out by the pasture and rejoined the track over the bridge to his own land, hidden from us by the barn. You remember the mood he was in when you brought him back, Wal. He was wound up tight. Then he seemed to relax. That could have been when he realized that nobody'd seen him.'

'Not at all bad,' Wallace said. He looked at the clock. 'One other suspect and then we'll have to go. Some of us have to work in the morning. Well, perhaps one more dram if you twist my arm.'

'Who's your suspect?' Ronnie asked.

'Simon.'

'Me?' I said. 'How do you make that out?'

'Old Murdo tried to blame Boss last winter when some of his sheep were savaged. It rankled.'

'Not particularly,' I said. 'He'd already described the culprit to the police as a collie, so everybody knew that it was only his spite coming out.'

'It rankled,' Wallace said firmly. 'Today, you came across a flattened pellet, one of Young Murdo's, while we were cleaning the rabbits and you slipped it into your pocket, either with evil intent or just as a keepsake.'

I decided to play along. 'Or just to reduce the amount of lead in the environment,' I said.

'You do slip things into your pockets all the time,' Alice said, 'whenever some small thing triggers an idea for a story. I usually put them on the corner of the desk when I empty your pockets.' I looked at her sharply but she was laughing at me.

'A wife can't give evidence against her husband,' I said comfortably. 'That's because fifty per cent of them would jump at any chance to get rid of the old man even if it entailed a little perjury.'

'There you are,' said Wallace. 'Not long after that, the old boy fell down in a faint or a heart attack or something. His wife ran out to him, thought he was dead and fainted. You came round the corner and saw your opportunity. Don't attempt to deny it.'

'I wasn't,' I said.

'Duggie was intent on his work. His cordless electric drill was within your reach. You grabbed it up, ran to the unconscious couple, drilled a hole through Old Murdo's skull and used the drill to push the pellet in.'

'Then what did I do with the drill?' I asked him.

'Scooted it along the ground into the barn.'

Ronnie shook his head. 'It was up on Duggie's scaffolding. I saw it.'

Wal waved away the objection as mere nit-picking. 'Then you used his hammer and a nail. I noticed the hammer on the floor of the barn later and thought it must have fallen off Duggie's plank. You pulled the nail out again and pushed it into the ground. Or, even better, into one of the rabbits so that you could carry it away. Ian searched everything else but he never searched the rabbits. Keep an eye on him, Alice, and make sure that he doesn't recover a nail while he's skinning them.'

'Well, if that's what I did,' I said, 'the pathologist should be able to prove it. A bullet hole's quite different from a nail-hole. Isn't it?' I asked Ronnie.

'Not to notice,' Ronnie said. 'I mind, away back, I worked a while in the slaughterhouse. The men didn't think much of the humane killer. Cartridges cost money and they preferred the old ways. After, they'd knock a hole through the skull with a six-inch nail in case the inspector came to check.'

'And I think that that's quite enough nonsense for one night,' Alice said briskly. 'You can leave the jeep where it is. I'll get the car out and run the two of you home, while you, Simon, go off to bed. Stay awake until I get back.'

With the house to myself (and the two sleeping babes) I sat down at the word processor. But the keys danced about in front of my eyes and the screen brightened and darkened until I felt faintly nauseous. I let Boss out into the garden for a minute and then went to bed. Luckily, the children slept on and the house did not catch fire, because I was sound asleep before Alice returned.

FIVE

In the morning, apart from a slight tendency to fall over if I stooped suddenly, I felt better than I had any right to expect. Alice was very understanding. Many wives would have objected to a husband who spent the evening at home boozing and bandying gruesome theories with his friends, but she regards the ability to take an occasional skinful of barley brew, especially of the malt variety, as being the mark of a true Scot and thus helping to merge me, the expatriate Sassenach, among those whom she considers to be real, proper people.

In a fit of conscience, I sat down to complete my typing for Ian. I expected him to arrive at any moment in search of his statements, but I was left in peace and, despite the dancing of the keys which only abated very slowly, I made good progress. I even added a synopsis, carefully phrased to avoid the danger of a libel suit if it should ever fall into the wrong hands, of our discussion after Ian's departure. After no little thought, I included Wal's theory about my own opportunity.

My printer was making zipping noises while I picked at a light lunch in the kitchen when the first message of impatience arrived, borne by the attractive WDC White. She was also carrying a shorthand book. She boggled slightly at the state of my workroom – my approach to time and motion study begins with the sensible notion that if something falls on the floor it is better left there until needed or it may only fall down again. As long as I know where everything is, that's tidy enough.

It took no more than a few minutes to discover and explain any differences between my word processor and the one she was used to. When the printer had done its stuff I gathered up my papers, allocated her a floppy disk and left her to it. As an afterthought, I returned to warn her that if she succumbed to a female urge to tidy anything I would make a complaint of harassment against her.

Boss had been short-changed in the matter of morning walks, so I took him along with me. The jeep had gone from the road, which suggested that either Ronnie or Wallace was up and about and, rightly or wrongly, felt fit to drive. The day was perfect. The rain had driven away the heavy heat, leaving cool sunshine to bless the landscape and dry the crops ready for harvesting. But for the shadow of death and the aftermath of the night before, it would have been a day for running barefoot through the grass or reading poetry aloud.

I descended the steps with care because my sense of balance was still less than perfect. When I looked up I saw that two young cyclists had stopped on the grass verge under a rowan tree and were engaged in earnest discussion. Blinking away the brightness of the sun, I recognized Sheila McKee and Young Murdo.

This was no surprise. The place was midway between their respective farm roads and I had sometimes noticed a very young couple trysting there without troubling myself over their identities. This time, however, instead of the tentative flirtations of youth, the touching of hands and even the stealing of an occasional kiss, they were a yard apart and their figures were stiff, their movements jerky. I guessed that there was an argument in progress. As I turned towards them, the girl jumped onto her bike and came pedalling past me. I saw that her face was twisted as if in distress and she was blinking hard.

Young Murdo let his bicycle fall. He stood looking after her. He seemed quite unaware of my approach. As I came level with him, I saw that tears were running down his cheeks. Boys on the verge of manhood hate to be seen crying. I would have passed by, pretending not to have noticed anything untoward, but Boss, who had always been his friend, recognized his distress, broke away from heel and licked the boy's hand.

Young Murdo came out of his trance, looked at me in horror and turned his back, feeling in vain for a handkerchief and then wiping his eyes with his shirt sleeve.

I felt almost as saddened. First love is beautiful to the beholder. The agony when it fails can be hard for the victim to bear. It was difficult to decide what to say, but I had to offer him some kind of comfort. 'Cheer up,' I said fatuously. 'She'll come round.'

He shook his head violently. 'Never,' he said throatily. 'It's done.'

'Women don't give up their dreams easily,' I said, speaking from long and sometimes bitter experience. 'She'll make it up sooner or later. Or, if not . . . Somewhere, there's a girl walking around with your name on an invisible label around her neck. She'll pop up just when you least expect her.' It was the best I could do. It was not enough, but I have asked myself since whether anything would have been enough.

He started to say something that came out as only an inarticulate sound of pain, then grabbed up his bicycle, swung a leg over and pedalled furiously off towards Easter Coullie. As I crossed the pasture I could see him on the farm road, still racing as fast as his old-fashioned machine would let him, until he vanished among the farm buildings.

Did Young Murdo have a rival, I wondered? In its usual haphazard manner, my mind turned aside into reverie. The scenario that had looked so promising the previous day would not work. The book would be one of the many that I had conceived but lost, stillborn. It was a pity. I had the perfect title. *Eternal Quadrangle*. But duality is the very essence of love and sex. There can only be a pair of opposites. Large and small. Hard and soft. The ball and the ring. Innocent and guilty.

I came back to reality. As nearly as I could judge, I was where I had been when I last saw Old Murdo alive. Walking normally, I timed myself to the corner of the barn. My best estimate was that he had been out of my sight for a minute and a quarter. Not very long; but many of the world's greatest crimes have been committed in less time. A minute is a long time in the dentist's chair.

The farmyard was both more orderly and less busy than when I had last seen it. The place where the body had been was still fenced off and a taped outline showed where it had lain after Mrs Heminson and I – with Duggie's help – had finished moving it around. But it seemed that work in that area had finished. At the barn, Duggie's scaffold and tools were still in place but there was no sign of the builder, who, I guessed, had been banished rather than arrested.

The large caravan was emplaced where the police cars had parked the day before. Temporary wires and cables trailed to it. Two police cars were squeezed into the remainder of that side of the yard and Ian was closing the door of one of them on Ronnie, who was seated like royalty, alone in the rear. The car pulled out. Ronnie bowed and waved graciously as he went by.

'If I'd known that you were chauffeuring your expert witnesses around,' I said, 'I'd have phoned for a car.'

Ian frowned. 'His alcohol count of milligrams per millilitre of blood won't get down into double figures before about Wednesday,' he said. 'I'm not having him drive around in that state while I might be coming the other way. Nor you, either,' he added severely. 'I have no objection to breathalyzing my

96

friends, so don't take any silly chances. Come on in.'

I said nothing, not wanting to start him wondering who had collected the jeep from my door. I settled Boss in the shade of the caravan and followed Ian up the steps.

The caravan had evidently been permanently converted for use as a mobile incident room. The one desk, the filing cabinets and the L-shaped table seemed to be fixtures and the walls were finished with pinboard already spattered with maps, charts and duty rosters. The table space was allocated to six workspaces but only one was occupied, by a very young constable who was listening to a telephone and making notes in longhand. The windows seemed to be sealed closed, presumably to prevent delicate discussions being overheard, and a small fan in the roof failed to cope with the stuffiness of the atmosphere.

The chairs were metal, swivel, typists for the use of. Ian took a seat behind the desk and nodded to the chair that was placed opposite for interviewees. I handed over my printouts.

'Your young lady's hard at work on my word processor,' I said.

'As long as she doesn't start gossiping with Alice.'

'She thinks I'm a slob.'

'She could be right.' Ian skimmed rapidly through the pages. He took longer over my summary of our discussion in his absence. 'Of course, I got most of this from Ronnie this morning,' he said, 'only not quite so methodically expressed. You can take your break now, Hodges.'

The young constable left the caravan. Evidently the minions were not going to hear the boss being indiscreet.

'Was Ronnie any help?' I asked.

'As helpful as he could be, which means not a damn bit. If the rain had come before the murder we could probably have solved the case by studying the traces. But people had been moving around, mostly quite legitimately, on baked ground –

97

and the rain followed afterwards. Hopeless. Mrs Heminson could have gone round the house on a pogo-stick before the rain fell and the signs would be lost by now. I'm not even expecting much from Forensic Science. After all, everyone who was around the farm that day had been around a hundred times before.

'When we went to look at the place where he'd found Young Murdo's bits and pieces, Ronnie did manage to point out that the far corner of the rape had been disturbed during the night, but whether it means anything or not we can't tell. He's sure that it wasn't like that when we passed it at the finish of shooting, and I think he's right.'

'A fox going after a rabbit?' I suggested.

'Ronnie thought not.' Ian tapped my notes with a finger and half smiled. 'At the moment, I'm gathering information rather than theorizing, but I think that we can exonerate you and discount several of the more fanciful ideas. A preliminary report from the pathologist came through by hand. The full autopsy will have to wait, probably until tonight, but he managed to get a scan which showed up the track of the bullet. No abnormal signs, as of the projectile being pushed around in the brain matter. So he went ahead with the first steps.' Ian picked up a thin sheaf of papers. ' "No traces of soot on hair or scalp . . . no muzzle imprint . . . incision through scalp . . . no soot or propellant residues on undersurface of scalp or outer surface of skull . . ." In fact, all he's saying is that the shot wasn't fired from less than three or four feet—'

'Or that it was fired from an air weapon,' I said.

'He makes that point. Not that there was much likelihood of the shot having been fired from close to. Where was I? Yes. " . . . hole in skull examined and measured . . . skull cap sawn, removed and examined . . . hole in outer surface smaller than hole in inner surface, typical of entry wound . . . dura mater removed to expose brain proper . . . brain removed and placed in solution of formaldehyde to harden by fixation . . ." The interesting bits come at the end. "Measurement of the metal projectile from X-ray photographs suggested that it was still expanding by flattening as it progressed through the skull and that its present diameter would not pass through the entry hole in the outer surface of the skull. This was later confirmed experimentally." '

'He was shot, then,' I said.

'There's more. "At the point of entry, the skull was of at least average thickness and would not have been penetrated by a pellet of conventional eight to ten foot-pounds energy." Which seems to take us right back to square one.'

'A souped-up airgun or a two-two rifle with a blank as propellant,' I said.

'Yes. That seemed to make the track of the projectile less critical, so the pathologist went ahead and recovered the pellet. A conventional waisted two-two airgun slug. Some signs of rifling marks, he thinks, but probably too damaged for the rifling and other marks to be matched to a weapon. I wish my revered father-in-law was here,' Ian said peevishly. 'Deborah phoned last night, but Keith's involved in some damned gundog competition. He'll get away as soon as he can.'

'Or as soon as he wants to,' I said.

'How true. It may come to a delicate balance between how much he's enjoying himself at the Game Fair against how much fun he expects to get out of stirring things up around here.

'There was one other snippet in the pathologist's report. The scan showed a serious brain tumour, possibly malignant.'

The implications took a few seconds to sort themselves out. I went for the easy one first. 'That probably explains Old Murdo's behaviour for the past year. He was a sour sort of devil when I first met him, but he was getting rapidly worse.'

Ian nodded. 'Very probably it does. He'd been complaining to his doctor of headaches but he refused to go for a scan, let alone a biopsy. Probably afraid of what he might find out.'

'From what I heard, he firmly believed that people only went into hospital to die. If he was going to pop his clogs anyway . . . ?'

'That doesn't make a damn bit of difference in law. We're all going to die, the only open question being when. If somebody falls off a cliff and you shoot him while he's on the way down, it's still murder.'

Ian paused and scowled around the contents of the caravan. 'I wanted to clear this one up quickly. I reported that an accidental death seemed very unlikely indeed. A chief inspector's been assigned to take over. He'll be here on Monday. For the moment, I'm reporting to him by phone. He's said to be clearing his desk, but if I know him he's getting ready for a golfing weekend.'

I could see the cause of Ian's concern. 'So it's a race. If he's here by the time you solve the case, he gets the credit,' I suggested.

'That's the way it goes. I've got men out scouring the countryside for possible witnesses, but I'm not very hopeful. Mrs Heminson's out of sedation now but doesn't seem able to add anything to the bones of what she said yesterday.' Ian frowned. 'All right,' he said suddenly. 'I'll break my own rule, but this is in confidence, mind. I know I can count on that. You never waste words in gossip if you can save them up for use in print. If it wasn't for one factor, Mrs Heminson would be my best suspect.'

'If you think she'd have the technical ability,' I said.

Ian leaned back as far as the chair would let him and looked at the ceiling of the caravan. I guessed that he was helped by being able to think aloud with somebody who would not be deterred by his seniority from arguing with him. 'One thing

100

you can never assume is a lack of knowledge. She might easily have seen her sons trying out the combination of a humane-killer cartridge and an airgun pellet. The sons deny that they've ever done any such thing, but that's only to be expected.

'All right, let's theorize for a minute or two. The timing is critical. We found the two-two rifle standing behind the back door. It had been recently fired and then cleaned, but Old Murdo had been shooting rabbits near the farm buildings that morning.'

'You're sure of that?' I asked.

'Duggie Bracken confirms it. The question is, could his wife have shot him from a window of the house and had time to clean the gun before running outside? She certainly never had a chance later.'

I tried to imagine an inexperienced woman – my guess was that Mrs Heminson was inexperienced with firearms – carrying out a minimal clean of a small-bore rifle. 'My guess would be no,' I said. 'I timed myself this morning. From the time I saw Old Murdo disappear until Mrs Heminson appeared would have been about one minute, give or take. And he wasn't even shot where I saw him. Allow time for him to walk another twenty yards and, no, I don't think that even a practised rifleman could have cleaned the gun, washed – because there was no oil on her hands – and run outside in the time. And her faint seemed absolutely genuine.'

Ian's face registered doubt. 'A faint is the easiest thing in the world to fake,' he said. 'You'd be amazed how many shoplifters try it on. None of us thought to stick a pin in her. The doctors claimed to recognize the classic symptoms of shock, but they often see what they expect to see.' Ian scratched his neck, his usual mannerism when deep in thought. 'Brett could have cleaned the rifle after his mother used it.'

'That assumes that not less than two thirds of his family was conspiring to murder him,' I pointed out. 'And presumably his wife at least had some idea that he was a dying man. His doctor must have warned him that he might have a tumour.'

Ian ignored my remarks. 'If Brett shot his father and she ran outside and fainted over the body, would she, when she came round, still be quick-witted enough to cover up for him?'

'I doubt it,' I said. 'But as well as the kitchen window there's a staircase window looking out onto the yard. She might not have seen Brett at all.'

Ian was nodding. 'He came in by the back door, went halfway up the stairs and shot his dad from the window. His mother, at the kitchen window, took the sound of the shot for Duggie Bracken's nail-gun but she saw her husband fall and ran outside. Brett cleaned the rifle, replaced it behind the door and hurried out through the garden and back to the tractor. I suppose it's possible. The cleaning gear's kept in a small room off the back passage. Brett's fingerprints are on it, of course, but he says that he cleaned the rifle after his father used it.

'So Brett is a definite possibility. Your other prime choice was Ken McKee.' Ian paused, took another look at my notes and scratched his neck again.

'What sticks in my craw,' I said, 'despite what I said in my notes, is the idea of either of the McKees wandering around on open land or heading for the house without being seen.'

'If one of them was there, we'll probably find that he or she was seen,' Ian told me. 'In my experience, you've only got to stop for a pee or leave a gate open on farmland and a dozen pairs of eyes are on you, but if you break your ankle or get treed by the bull there's nobody for miles.'

That much was true. 'It's a pity,' I said, 'that I was with you instead of at home. When I'm at work I'm looking over this area every time I raise my eyes.'

Ian registered mild amusement. 'The way you go into a trance when you're working, I don't suppose you'd have noticed a herd of hairy elephants stampeding across the landscape, let alone remembered a solitary figure hoofing it between the fields.'

That mild stricture, I had to admit, was true. 'I have one fresh scrap of information for you,' I said. I told him about the emotional scene between Young Murdo and Sheila McKee. 'It occurred to me that her distress might have been because she saw her father kill Old Murdo. She spends a lot of time on that knoll on the boundary.'

Ian sat up straight. 'Or it could have been because Young Murdo saw Ken McKee do the deed.'

'That would square with your theory that somebody always sees the rural miscreant,' I said.

He waved my comment aside as frivolous. 'I'm beginning to fancy Ken McKee for this,' he said. 'Assuming that he turns out to have an air cane of the right calibre he had the means, plus a possible opportunity and the father and mother of a motive. His daughter may have the key. I'll see that young lady before the day's much older, but I doubt if she'll incriminate her dad.'

His mention of the passing time reminded me. 'Alice says to come for a meal this evening,' I said. 'You won't have time to cook for yourself.'

'Thank her for me, but I have to go in to Edinburgh this evening to report in person. Tomorrow, if Deborah isn't back by then?'

'Tomorrow, then,' I said. 'Have the press been onto it yet?'

'We had a few phone-calls, but by good luck they came while there still seemed to be a probability of the death being accidental. We told them that it was being treated as such, which was more or less true, and I haven't felt obliged to issue a correction. There may be a line or two in tomorrow's papers.'

'They'll give you a hammering when they find out you've been holding back a hot story.'

Ian produced a semblance of his usual cheerful grin. 'By

that time, my superior will be here to answer for it. Or if not, I'll blame him anyway.'

We were interrupted by two officers who came into the caravan and sat down at the table. Ian immediately became the formal police inspector. 'Thank you very much, Mr Parbitter,' he said. 'You've been very helpful. We'll get in touch with you again if there are any more questions.' A wink behind his subordinates' backs softened the words.

I was glad to escape from the heat that was building up in the caravan and into the welcome breeze outside. Boss got up to join me as I descended the steps, relieved to see me again but in no hurry to get moving. He was still stiff after his labours of the day before. While I waited for him to finish a cautious stretch of each limb in turn, I looked around me. Duggie's tools seemed to be much more neatly arranged than when he had left them.

From where I was standing, I could see the smaller yard that ran along to the back door and the tap and hose with which Miss Mather had been trying to cleanse the Augean car. There was a bush of dark red roses beyond, which would have clashed horribly with the car's colour. But there was no sign of the small DAF. Surely she couldn't be driving around in it? Or had it been removed for examination of its contents back at the police garage?

Standing there with all the crucial places in sight, I found that I was unconvinced. The theories I had been discussing were credible as theories and yet I could not give credence to any one of them. My opinions were subjective and yet I knew that I was right. It was as though the tiny missile had come out of thin air – which, of course, it had. But there was something else, something that we were missing. A dim memory from long, long ago was moving like a fish below the water, refusing to rise to my lure.

Ian and one of the constables came out of the caravan. Ian

nodded to me. They got into one of the cars and drove off. The McKees, I decided, were about to receive visitors.

There was nothing to do but go home. My curiosity was still a-tingle and as the finder of the two inert bodies I felt an almost proprietary interest. If I thought about something else, perhaps the memory would surface. When WDC White had finished, I could retrieve her work from the memory of my word processor and have a look at any fresh reports, including Jean Mather's statement.

Brett Heminson was crossing the yard towards the house and I remembered that I had not had a chance to offer the few obligatory words of condolence. He was in working clothes, but he struck me as unusually neat and clean until I realized that the police would have taken away all his clothing of the previous day.

He altered course to meet me, stooping to give Boss a pat. 'Hi there, old fellow,' he said. 'Afternoon, Mr Parbitter.' His smile was absent but otherwise he was his usual placid self. There was blood on his hands and I felt a jolt of horror until it came to me that he would have been cutting up for mutton the ewe that Miss Mather had put down.

For some reason, white lies stick in my throat. None of the customary platitudes would come out, simply because not one of them would have had any truth in it. The fact that Old Murdo had been the victim of a pathological disorder excused his malignancy without altering the fact. 'I'm sorry,' I said. He could decide for himself what I was sorry about.

He nodded. 'You'll come in for a minute?'

'I won't be keeping you?'

'This is the slack time. There's nothing urgent until we can start harvesting. Yesterday's rain set everything back.'

As I followed him indoors, I thought that a murder might also have had some delaying effect. Old Murdo had not been inclined towards hospitality and I had never been inside the house before. The sitting room was colourless, furnished economically but with an eye to comfort and very well kept. An ornate clock ticked loudly above the empty fireplace. Boss subsided on a hearthrug of gaudy pattern. The clock on the mantelpiece was flanked by a pair of the china dogs that are becoming collectors' items.

'You'll take a dram?' Brett asked.

Old Murdo had liked his dram but his taste would have run to the youngest and cheapest of the blended whiskies. After the previous evening's excesses, my stomach burned at the very thought. I decided to break with local custom.

'I could manage a beer,' I said.

He seemed pleased. I was left alone for a minute while Brett went to wash and I wondered whether some of his father's parsimony had rubbed off on him. He returned and poured a beer apiece and we sat on either side of the hearth.

'How's your mother taking it?' I asked.

'Better than you'd think, now that she's over the shock. I'm fetching her home this afternoon.'

'That's rather soon, isn't it?'

'Aye, it is,' he said. 'I'd rather she stayed until we had the place to ourselves again. But that could be long enough. They're out of the house now, except for sharing the kitchen. And at least they've brought their own milk and tea. We'll get by. She's set her heart on getting home and sorting us out. She's got more spunk than many of us, my Mam.'

Was it spunk, I wondered, or were there some loose ends Mrs Heminson was in a hurry to tidy away?

He went on speaking affectionately of his mother. A picture began to emerge, of a matriarchal but motherly woman, wise and yet tender, which I found hard to relate to the large, tough battleaxe of her reputation. Soon my mind wandered. How had my mother looked to the stranger? I was also wondering whether I dared ask Brett how he thought his father had been

106

Sir Peter was not deterred. 'Then we'll walk,' he said.

Boss was walking stiffly. I sent him to lie in the barn and told him to stay there. We set off across the pasture and cut round the back of the farm buildings. Nothing was said, but we seemed to walk faster and faster. I was soon panting, but Sir Peter seemed to keep up effortlessly with Brett, who was breaking into a trot.

When we came to the bridge, we saw Murdo. He seemed to be down on his knees and peering into one of the rabbit holes, but at a second glance I saw that his head was deep in the hole so that his shoulders sealed it.

Brett gave an inarticulate groan and broke into a run, descending the side of the gully in one leaping slither and jumping the stream. When I caught up with him, he had already pulled his brother's head free. He gathered him up in his arms. Under the sandy dirt, Murdo looked very young, very pink and white.

Sir Peter arrived, panting. 'Leave him,' he said. 'Leave him. He's dead.'

'No.' Brett looked older, so much older that the resemblance to his dead father was almost frightening. He turned away and splashed through the stream, then turned the body over one shoulder so that he had a hand with which to help himself up the bank. At the top, he broke into a run again along the track. I could barely keep up with him. For a short while I thought that he was right and that Murdo was still alive, but then I realized that what I had taken for groans were no more than the air being bounced out of the dead boy's lungs. The regular sounds were more than I could bear. I slowed to a walk. Brett drew away and Sir Peter overtook me.

When we reached the corner of the barn, the body had been laid neatly beside the caravan. The three officers had emerged and Brett was imploring them for help. One of them ran to the nearest police car.

killed or whereabouts he himself had been just before the murder, whether he had seen any strangers in the fields, whether he and Young Murdo had ever experimented at firing airgun slugs out of the .22 rifle, whether he had known that his father had a tumour, or any one of a dozen other things.

Before I could formulate any acceptable questions, there was a ring at the doorbell.

'I'll see who it is,' Brett said quickly. 'You bide there.'

He left me with the tick of the clock and my unasked questions for company. I heard voices at the door and Brett returned, followed by the sticklike figure of Sir Peter Hay. The old boy seemed to have tidied himself up, at least to the extent of brushing out his hair and wearing a less tattered kilt than usual. But, of course, I remembered as I got up, the call would be formal.

'Don't go, my dear chap,' Sir Peter said to me. 'I've just been giving Brett my condolences. Bad business, eh?'

'Terrible,' I said. Brett grunted. Boss, subsiding again at my feet, echoed him.

Sir Peter evidently shared my distrust of Old Murdo's taste in whisky. He accepted a beer and lowered his skinny frame carefully into one of the chairs. He was much more adept than I was at uttering conventional platitudes without ever quite saying that Old Murdo would be greatly missed.

'The other reason I came,' he said suddenly, 'was to ask what you intend to do. But maybe it's too early for that?'

'It's early days, right enough,' Brett said. 'When I saw Mam, she was talking as though we'd be staying on. It was as if all she wanted was to get life back to where it was before, as near as it can be. The most I could say just now is that I think we'll be wanting to keep the farm on . . . if we're let.'

Sir Peter nodded his thinning, silver curls. 'That's really all I wanted to know. If you and your mother feel that you can manage the place, the tenancy's yours. You'll have Young

Murdo to help, of course. Or Murdo, as I suppose we'll have to learn to call him.'

For the first time since I had known him, Brett was looking flustered. 'Can we speak again, Sir Peter, once we can . . . see our way past this business?'

Sir Peter looked genuinely astonished. 'But surely . . . A stray bullet from a long way off, I was given to understand. That's the word that's doing the rounds. Or perhaps a poacher?'

'Maybe,' Brett said. 'I surely to God hope so. I've no more idea than you have, but the police were asking some dashed funny questions. I can't make head nor tail of it, but I'm sorely fashed and that's the truth.'

'That's the way the police are. It's their job to poke and pry. But you'll find' – Sir Peter leaned forward and shook an earnest finger, ignoring my attempt at a warning look – 'mark my words, there'll be a simple explanation. I can't believe . . . But we'll say no more about it until the police have done their stuff and the Fiscal's enquiry's been and gone.' He sat back, satisfied that he had set the other's mind at rest. 'And then, what will your plans be? Do you still hope to go to Agricultural College? There's not the fat in farming that there used to be, but there's still a good living to be made if you're up to date.'

Brett sighed, relaxing slowly. 'Murdo and Mam would be hard put to it to manage,' he said. 'It's Murdo will have to go to the College.'

'You'll be disappointed, but I can see the sense in what you're saying. Where is Murdo, by the way? And how's he taking it?'

'I don't know what to make of him,' Brett said. 'He's in one of his moods. You ken how he is. And I can't blame him. They were close until Dad started with the headaches. After that, Murdo couldn't seem to do a thing right and Dad was

108

hard on him, very hard. Dad's death's been a shock to [...] right.' Brett frowned into the dead fireplace for a minut[e...] he tried to plumb his brother's feelings. 'My guess,' [...] at last, 'is that it's come as a relief to him and he feel[s...] for feeling that way. Does that make sense?'

'Not an uncommon reaction,' Sir Peter said.

'And then seeing Mam take it so hard. It seemed t[o...] keep him busy. He's away down finishing off the rabb[it...] that were left yesterday.'

It was a few seconds before his words sank in. Th[en...] myself jump. 'How could he?' I asked. 'He left th[e...] Cymag and Ronnie picked it up.'

'That was a new tin. There was a bittie left in the [...] enough to do the few holes that still needed.'

I felt an unease in my guts. 'I don't think you sho[uld...] left him running around with the makings for pois[on...] said. 'Sheila McKee broke up with him this m[orning...] seemed to knock the last of the stuffing out of him.[...]'

'It would,' Sir Peter said. 'Those two have been sw[eet...] since they were in primary school together.'

'No,' Brett said, mostly to himself. 'Surely not.' [...] at the clock. 'He'd surely never make away of hi[mself...] the girl. Not when he knows how it would upset ou[r...]

'Shouldn't he be back by now?' I asked.

'I'll see if he isn't in the yard.'

We followed Brett out. Sir Peter's Land Rover a[nd...] police car were crammed in beside the caravan and [...] now three heads to be seen behind the caravan [...] Otherwise the scene was unchanged.

'Murdo!' Brett shouted. There was an echo but [...]

'We'll all be easier in our minds once we've se[en the...] boy's all right,' Sir Peter said. 'Hop in the Land R[over...]

'Better not,' Brett said. 'The police have a tape a[...] don't want any vehicles past there yet.'

109

'Where are you going?' Brett shouted after him.

'We need a doctor and an ambulance. It'll be quicker by radio. Take Mr Heminson into the house,' he told one of his colleagues. They knew as well as I did that both the Murdos were dead.

But Brett stood, looking down at his brother. Only when the officer who was using the radio began to relay the news to Ian, putting the tragedy into clumsy words, did Brett seem ready to turn away.

At that moment Boss came out of the barn. He sniffed the body. I jumped forward to pull him away in case any trace of cyanide gas still lingered about the boy. But just then Boss sat back on his haunches, threw back his grizzled head and began to howl.

Brett bolted into the house.

killed or whereabouts he himself had been just before the murder, whether he had seen any strangers in the fields, whether he and Young Murdo had ever experimented at firing airgun slugs out of the .22 rifle, whether he had known that his father had a tumour, or any one of a dozen other things.

Before I could formulate any acceptable questions, there was a ring at the doorbell.

'I'll see who it is,' Brett said quickly. 'You bide there.'

He left me with the tick of the clock and my unasked questions for company. I heard voices at the door and Brett returned, followed by the sticklike figure of Sir Peter Hay. The old boy seemed to have tidied himself up, at least to the extent of brushing out his hair and wearing a less tattered kilt than usual. But, of course, I remembered as I got up, the call would be formal.

'Don't go, my dear chap,' Sir Peter said to me. 'I've just been giving Brett my condolences. Bad business, eh?'

'Terrible,' I said. Brett grunted. Boss, subsiding again at my feet, echoed him.

Sir Peter evidently shared my distrust of Old Murdo's taste in whisky. He accepted a beer and lowered his skinny frame carefully into one of the chairs. He was much more adept than I was at uttering conventional platitudes without ever quite saying that Old Murdo would be greatly missed.

'The other reason I came,' he said suddenly, 'was to ask what you intend to do. But maybe it's too early for that?'

'It's early days, right enough,' Brett said. 'When I saw Mam, she was talking as though we'd be staying on. It was as if all she wanted was to get life back to where it was before, as near as it can be. The most I could say just now is that I think we'll be wanting to keep the farm on . . . if we're let.'

Sir Peter nodded his thinning, silver curls. 'That's really all I wanted to know. If you and your mother feel that you can manage the place, the tenancy's yours. You'll have Young

107

Murdo to help, of course. Or Murdo, as I suppose we'll have to learn to call him.'

For the first time since I had known him, Brett was looking flustered. 'Can we speak again, Sir Peter, once we can ... see our way past this business?'

Sir Peter looked genuinely astonished. 'But surely ... A stray bullet from a long way off, I was given to understand. That's the word that's doing the rounds. Or perhaps a poacher?'

'Maybe,' Brett said. 'I surely to God hope so. I've no more idea than you have, but the police were asking some dashed funny questions. I can't make head nor tail of it, but I'm sorely fashed and that's the truth.'

'That's the way the police are. It's their job to poke and pry. But you'll find' – Sir Peter leaned forward and shook an earnest finger, ignoring my attempt at a warning look – 'mark my words, there'll be a simple explanation. I can't believe ... But we'll say no more about it until the police have done their stuff and the Fiscal's enquiry's been and gone.' He sat back, satisfied that he had set the other's mind at rest. 'And then, what will your plans be? Do you still hope to go to Agricultural College? There's not the fat in farming that there used to be, but there's still a good living to be made if you're up to date.'

Brett sighed, relaxing slowly. 'Murdo and Mam would be hard put to it to manage,' he said. 'It's Murdo will have to go to the College.'

'You'll be disappointed, but I can see the sense in what you're saying. Where is Murdo, by the way? And how's he taking it?'

'I don't know what to make of him,' Brett said. 'He's in one of his moods. You ken how he is. And I can't blame him. They were close until Dad started with the headaches. After that, Murdo couldn't seem to do a thing right and Dad was hard on him, very hard. Dad's death's been a shock to him all right.' Brett frowned into the dead fireplace for a minute while he tried to plumb his brother's feelings. 'My guess,' he said at last, 'is that it's come as a relief to him and he feels guilty for feeling that way. Does that make sense?'

'Not an uncommon reaction,' Sir Peter said.

'And then seeing Mam take it so hard. It seemed better to keep him busy. He's away down finishing off the rabbit holes that were left yesterday.'

It was a few seconds before his words sank in. Then I felt myself jump. 'How could he?' I asked. 'He left the tin of Cymag and Ronnie picked it up.'

'That was a new tin. There was a bittie left in the old one, enough to do the few holes that still needed.'

I felt an unease in my guts. 'I don't think you should have left him running around with the makings for poison gas,' I said. 'Sheila McKee broke up with him this morning. It seemed to knock the last of the stuffing out of him.'

'It would,' Sir Peter said. 'Those two have been sweethearts since they were in primary school together.'

'No,' Brett said, mostly to himself. 'Surely not.' He looked at the clock. 'He'd surely never make away of himself over the girl. Not when he knows how it would upset our Mam.'

'Shouldn't he be back by now?' I asked.

'I'll see if he isn't in the yard.'

We followed Brett out. Sir Peter's Land Rover and another police car were crammed in beside the caravan and there were now three heads to be seen behind the caravan windows. Otherwise the scene was unchanged.

'Murdo!' Brett shouted. There was an echo but no answer.

'We'll all be easier in our minds once we've seen that the boy's all right,' Sir Peter said. 'Hop in the Land Rover.'

'Better not,' Brett said. 'The police have a tape across. They don't want any vehicles past there yet.'

109

Sir Peter was not deterred. 'Then we'll walk,' he said.

Boss was walking stiffly. I sent him to lie in the barn and told him to stay there. We set off across the pasture and cut round the back of the farm buildings. Nothing was said, but we seemed to walk faster and faster. I was soon panting, but Sir Peter seemed to keep up effortlessly with Brett, who was breaking into a trot.

When we came to the bridge, we saw Murdo. He seemed to be down on his knees and peering into one of the rabbit holes, but at a second glance I saw that his head was deep in the hole so that his shoulders sealed it.

Brett gave an inarticulate groan and broke into a run, descending the side of the gully in one leaping slither and jumping the stream. When I caught up with him, he had already pulled his brother's head free. He gathered him up in his arms. Under the sandy dirt, Murdo looked very young, very pink and white.

Sir Peter arrived, panting. 'Leave him,' he said. 'Leave him. He's dead.'

'No.' Brett looked older, so much older that the resemblance to his dead father was almost frightening. He turned away and splashed through the stream, then turned the body over one shoulder so that he had a hand with which to help himself up the bank. At the top, he broke into a run again along the track. I could barely keep up with him. For a short while I thought that he was right and that Murdo was still alive, but then I realized that what I had taken for groans were no more than the air being bounced out of the dead boy's lungs. The regular sounds were more than I could bear. I slowed to a walk. Brett drew away and Sir Peter overtook me.

When we reached the corner of the barn, the body had been laid neatly beside the caravan. The three officers had emerged and Brett was imploring them for help. One of them ran to the nearest police car.

'Where are you going?' Brett shouted after him.

'We need a doctor and an ambulance. It'll be quicker by radio. Take Mr Heminson into the house,' he told one of his colleagues. They knew as well as I did that both the Murdos were dead.

But Brett stood, looking down at his brother. Only when the officer who was using the radio began to relay the news to Ian, putting the tragedy into clumsy words, did Brett seem ready to turn away.

At that moment Boss came out of the barn. He sniffed the body. I jumped forward to pull him away in case any trace of cyanide gas still lingered about the boy. But just then Boss sat back on his haunches, threw back his grizzled head and began to howl.

Brett bolted into the house.

SIX

As any member of the police would confirm, they are often hampered because witnesses to any event, large or small, slip quietly away if they can. For this, the Force has only itself to blame. Professional men in the public sector often see the public as a flock of sheeplike creatures whose time is of no account compared to their own and, unaccountably, the public supports that view by allowing them to get away with it. The police like to consider themselves similarly privileged. Witnesses have to wait around to be interrogated, to sign statements and for their moment in court. A dead body, being in no hurry, takes precedence.

So Sir Peter and I were banished back to the sitting room while the routine of Police Surgeon, Pathologist, Scene of Crime Officers and Forensic Science Specialists again went into gear and ground as slowly as the mills of God but, I hoped, rather more effectively, while Brett, as next of kin and finder of the body, was put through his paces in the caravan.

This gave Sir Peter his first chance to allow his curiosity full rein. To pass the time, I gave him a detailed account of the events surrounding Old Murdo's death, answering his questions as best I could. While we spoke, I could see his curiosity giving way to distress. He dearly loved a mystery, but regarded all the local populace, and especially his tenantry and their families, as his personal babies.

Much later, when I had covered the facts, some of them more than once, and we were beginning to pick over the few tenable theories, each of which Sir Peter pronounced unthinkable, WDC White appeared at the door.

'Inspector Fellowes is coming to take your statements,' she said. In a similarly reverent tone might be said, 'The doctor will see you now.'

'Did you get on all right with my word processor?' I asked her.

She accepted the implied slur without comment. 'We arrived at an understanding,' she said.

'And you left it as you found it?'

Her nose lifted. 'I left it a lot cleaner than I found it,' she said. 'And I put a much needed new ribbon in your printer.'

Ian arrived before I could find a suitable reply. 'We may as well take you together,' he said. 'You may be able to refresh each other's memories.'

The lengthy process of taking statements began. Our accounts were virtually identical, except for my encounter with the boy that morning. When we had finished, Ian nodded to the WDC and she closed her shorthand book.

'Could you not have stopped Brett from moving the body and stirring up the scene?' Ian enquired severely.

'Not without resorting to violence,' Sir Peter said. 'He was in a state. And, after all, none of us is a medical man. The boy might just possibly have been alive.'

Ian shook his head. 'The doctors agree that he must have been dead for half an hour before he was found. Almost certainly the autopsy will confirm poisoning by whichever of the cyanide gases is produced by Cymag in contact with damp earth. Brett himself could have been killed, bending down to the hole and pulling his brother out. You didn't think of that?'

'In the heat of the moment,' I said, 'no, we didn't. And he'd already pulled him out before we caught up with him.' I

116

decided to push my luck. 'It didn't look like an accident.'

Ian hesitated and then decided in favour of frankness. 'Nor does it to us,' he said. 'For one thing, I'm advised that Cymag is activated by contact with the dampness in the earth. In dry conditions, that could have taken time. Somebody had scooshed water into the hole, using an empty tin that was lying nearby, before adding the Cymag. We opened up several of the other treated holes – very cautiously, I need hardly say – and none of them showed any such signs. No worthwhile prints on the tin.'

'A bad business,' said Sir Peter. 'Tell me, if you can – were there any marks of violence on the body?'

'There were some bruises, about a day old, probably inflicted by his father's stick.'

'That wasn't exactly what I meant,' Sir Peter pointed out gently.

'No,' Ian said. 'You want to know exactly what I want to know. Did somebody push his head into the burrow?'

'And did they?' I asked.

'You both seem to agree that his shirt looked clean and newly pressed. It would be difficult to manhandle even an unconscious person, let alone a struggling victim, into a position with his head down a rabbit hole without using his clothes as a grip. There were no suspicious marks on the flesh that we could see. But very often that's the way of it, if death took place before bruises had time to develop. The autopsy may answer the question.'

'A bad business,' Sir Peter said again. He waited but Ian made no comment. 'To come back to the earlier matter of the death of Old Murdo. Your men hadn't got around to speaking to me. In fact, they had no reason to believe that I knew anything of use. But I can confirm something that you may or may not know. I had no idea of its relevance until a few minutes ago.'

Ian nodded again to WDC White, who whipped open her book.

'Simon tells me that Old Murdo died yesterday at about five past one.'

'That's so,' Ian said. 'I reached the scene at about ten past.'

'From what Simon tells me, I surmise that Ken McKee may be under suspicion,' said Sir Peter, carefully avoiding any suggestion that he and I might have been discussing various locals as possible murderers. 'I got home for lunch at one. I tried to phone Ken McKee. A little matter of vermin he's failing to control. His wife tried to tell me that he wasn't in, but I could hear his voice in the background, shouting at his dog. That would have been between five and ten past.'

The clock ticked a dozen times before Ian spoke. 'Thank you,' he said. 'Is it all right if the WDC uses your machine again?' he asked me.

'I suppose so,' I said.

Miss White took the hint and left us.

Sir Peter stirred in his chair. 'Does that agree with what Ken McKee told you?'

'Ken McKee and his daughter have been less than co-operative,' Ian said. 'Up to the moment when I was called back here with the news of a second death, the girl was uttering nothing but sobs and her father was insisting that neither of them was going to say a word until Mr Enterkin the solicitor was present. McKee, in fact, might have been going out of his way to convince me of his own guilt.'

'Perhaps he was drawing attention away from his daughter,' I said. 'She could have borrowed her father's air cane. That could account for her tearfulness and her renunciation of Young Murdo.'

Sir Peter made another small mew of distress. Even at his age he still regarded young females as delicate blooms, more likely to be sinned against than sinning.

'I collected the air cane last night,' Ian said. 'Mr McKee's fingerprints were all over it and nobody else's. Not conclusive, of course, but it goes to support certain other evidence, not even including your own.'

'It begins to look very black for young Brett,' Sir Peter said sadly.

'It would,' Ian said, 'but for the other evidence I just mentioned. You know the farmhouse at Staundinstane?'

Sir Peter gave one of his short yaps of laughter. 'Know it? I can see it from here,' he said, nodding towards the window. 'What's more, I used to own the whole place. I sold it to an insurance company just before the price of farms did its nosedive,' he added with satisfaction. 'I kept the sporting rights, though.'

Leaning sideways, I could make out the upper half of a farmhouse that I had never known was there. It was small in the distance and peeped over the swell of the ground that hid it from Tansy House.

'The tenant's old mother lives upstairs,' said Ian. 'She's more or less confined to her room, without anything to keep her occupied except the window and the telly. I wouldn't wish that fate on anybody, but chairbound old folk are often our best witnesses.

'She had the one o'clock news on, but she wasn't very interested – there was nothing new on the bulletins. She was looking out of the window while she waited for *Neighbours* to come on. She could see Brett zigging and zagging around on the tractor, doing all the odd jobs, and nobody else was in sight.'

'Could she recognize Brett at that distance?' I asked.

'Probably not. But that doesn't matter, because there was nobody else driving a tractor around on Easter Coullie land.'

'You're sure of that?' asked Sir Peter.

'That there was only one tractor circulating? She's quite

119

adamant on that point. She says that, just before the mid-news summary came on, three figures walked along the track from the gully and soon afterwards whoever was on the tractor stopped it, stood up to look towards here and then came haring back to the farmyard, still on the tractor. That would be just about when Brett arrived. On the tractor.'

'Which leaves you without any suspects at all,' said Sir Peter.

'Except, possibly, Mrs Heminson. All the obvious and simple theories seem to be discounted,' Ian said gloomily. 'So it's back to square one again. Up the ladder and down the snake. What I have to do now is look for unlikely scenarios, assuming premeditation and complicity, while checking everybody's statements and timetables against Forensic's findings, looking for discrepancies and hoping against hope that my men on house-to-house enquiries can turn up yet another witness.'

'Sooner you than me,' I said. It seemed to be a moment when a little lightening of the atmosphere might be appreciated. 'There are sheep all over the place. Would the old lady have noticed if somebody had crawled across the ground wrapped in a sheepskin?'

Sir Peter snorted with suppressed laughter, but it was a measure of Ian's desperation that he took the suggestion seriously for a few seconds. We had to point out to him that such a disguise might have fooled an old lady half a mile away but it would not have deceived us, or Brett on his tractor, or Mrs Heminson at a window of the house.

Somebody, probably Brett, would have had to break the news to Mrs Heminson that, on top of being widowed, she had also lost her younger son. I was only glad that that duty did not fall to me. She took the news bravely, or so we were told, but although she had not suffered the suspected stroke her blood pressure was still high and it was decided to keep her for another night in the hospital. (Nothing remains secret for long in a small community when there is drama in the air, not even medical records.)

Alice could not bear the thought of Brett being left to fend for himself, alone in the farmhouse but for the comings and goings of any police still on duty and in need of the facilities. While I took Boss and the children for a walk through the wood behind Tansy House and up the hill, she drove to Easter Coullie and dragged the politely reluctant Brett back with her to share our evening meal.

He was not the most cheerful of company. He tried to interact with the children but they soon sensed that his heart wasn't in it and went more willingly than usual to their beds.

It would almost have been healthier, I felt, if Brett had let himself go and got plastered, but he refused all but the minimum of token drinks and worked hard to maintain polite conversation. Ronnie looked in during the evening but, finding neither drink nor gossip flowing, soon went on his way again.

Alice, ever warm of heart, offered Brett a bed – in the form of the couch in my study – for the night, but he refused. 'I maun be away home,' he said. 'The police have left the house a' tapsalteerie. Mam will be home the morn and it'll be less of a shock if she finds it clean and redded.' He paused and shook his head as though to dispel unwelcome images. 'Murdo was never meant to be happy,' he said. 'Even as a wee lad, when things went wrong for him he wouldn't scream or cry. He'd just go away into a world of his own and you couldn't get a word out of him. And if he got a gift or a treat that'd have sent another kid wild with joy he seemed to question it, as if he was wondering if it was what he really wanted. It seems to me that if you have to wonder if you're happy, you're not. Maybe young Sheila could've put some life into him, but

121

I don't know. Perhaps it's as well that they're away together, him and Dad. They'll be company, and surely Dad's left his headaches behind him.'

There was a quaver in his voice and I found myself with nothing to say.

'But can you manage on your own?' Alice asked. She has no great opinion of a man's ability to clean a house.

Brett cleared his throat. 'Aye,' he said briskly. 'Fine that. I'm a dab hand wi' a duster and I ken where things belong.' He paused, sensing our concern. 'I've slept in an empty house afore now,' he added.

I would not have cared to sleep alone in a house two of whose occupants had died in uncertain circumstances within the previous thirty-six hours, but perhaps writers suffer from an excess of imagination. We let him carry his sorrow away with him, on foot through bright moonlight, then shared the washing up and settled cosily in front of the television for what was left of the evening.

In the morning my mind was still full of the puzzle, but I could think of no excuse to go and try to extract the latest news from Ian. WDC White had taken with her the floppy disk containing her transcripts of the statements and when I tried to recover her material from the memory of the word processor I found that she had overlaid it with a mildly insulting message followed by a stream of gibberish.

The word processor seemed to be waiting for something. A record while my memory was fresh might be valuable later. It might also clarify my thinking. I recalled my original statement from the disk and began amplifying it into the full story that I knew I would write some day. I broke for lunch and returned to work. More and more detail, some probably irrelevant and some certainly not, came rushing back and I set it all down.

I had brought my account almost up to date when I awoke out of the drugged state that comes over me when I am writing

122

and I realized that a car had stopped in the road below. I stood up on my chair – the only way in which I can see over the rockery.

Most farmers do themselves well in the matter of cars, before tax and on the machinery account. But Old Murdo's cheese-paring had extended even into this area and it was his worn-out Lada that stood below. Mrs Heminson was struggling up the steps on Brett's arm.

Wondering to what on earth we could possibly owe the honour, I hurried to the front door and opened it as they reached the summit. Mrs Heminson's bulk was wrapped in a plain black dress which looked new. Brett was smarter than I had seen him, in a grey suit, white shirt and black tie.

Evidently this was a formal visit. I shook hands with them both and said sincerely how sorry I was about Young Murdo. About the boy's father, I paraphrased as best I could Sir Peter's well-chosen words as I led the way into the sitting room. Brett helped his mother lower herself into a substantial chair. She was a daunting figure, endowed with a square jaw, hooked nose and piercing eyes. Several moles sprouted hair. But she had courage and a dignity like that of a warrior after battle. Strip away the surplus flesh and the damage of the years and it was clear that she had never been beautiful but she might once have been a striking woman. It was not easy to imagine her in the arms of a younger version of Old Murdo.

Alice joined us. Her instinctive *savoir faire* carried her through. I could hear the kettle already coming to the boil. She stooped and kissed the woman's cheek. 'It's terrible for you,' she said. 'I'm so, so sorry.'

'Aye. Folk must die. That's the way of it. But it's hard when two go together.' She sighed. 'I was sure that my man was dead before I ran out of the house, but I couldn't stop myself.'

'How could you be sure?' I asked.

'I saw him go down,' she said simply. 'He didn't stop or stagger. He was walking and then he just went down on the instant, atween one step and the next, like a stag that's been—' She broke off.

'Would you like tea?' Alice asked quickly.

Mrs Heminson bowed gravely. Alice left me to deal with our guests. I was dumbstruck, but Mrs Heminson had her own code of proper behaviour. Evidently, any further discussion of how her two menfolk had died would be considered a breach of manners. She spoke about the weather and the harvest prospects until Alice came back with the trolley, laden with tea and small cakes.

I was no help during the exchanges that followed. The phrase 'Alice's tea-party' kept running through my mind.

At the end of a nicely judged twenty minutes, when Mrs Heminson was clearly preparing to take her leave, she came to the point at last. 'I called in to thank you,' she said. 'You were kind to Brett last night, just when he needed it most. It's aye a comfort to have good neighbours.'

'It was nothing,' Alice said. 'Nothing.'

'It was muckle. My man was doomed, he'd have been dead by the year's end. But the boy . . .'

The doors to the walled garden stood open in the fine weather. The children chose that moment to appear, Peter first and then Jane toddling after. They came to stand one either side of Alice and looked solemnly at the visitors. With the sunlight behind them, their hair shone like halos.

Mrs Heminson's large face began to break up. She put out a hand to Brett and he helped her to her feet. She would have said something but her voice had gone. She kissed us both and I felt the tears on her cheeks and the prickle of a stiff hair. At the front door, she found her voice and thanked us again.

'You'll be careful?' I said awkwardly. Even in her distressed state I found her as formidable as any of my aunts. 'It's only an assumption that your son . . . made away with himself.'

She shook her formidable head. 'This is the end of it,' she said firmly. 'It's the McKee lass I'm sorriest for. Well, if there's ever to be any grandchildren to carry on, they'll be Brett's. We can't say yet when the burials will be. Brett will let you ken.' She gave me a last, piercing look. 'You're no' to feel bad,' she said.

We stood at the top of the steps and waved until the car was out of sight. Anything less would have offended against the dignity that the farmer's widow had pulled around herself.

Back in the sitting room, Alice dropped into a chair. 'I could use a drink,' she said. 'A whisky.'

Alice never drinks spirits, but there are times when only a stiff drink will do. 'Me too,' I said. 'It never occurred to me that we might be bidden to the funerals.' I poured a dram for each of us. 'Can't we get out of it?'

She shook her head. 'We'll have to show respect.'

'That old biddy knows something,' I said.

'Yes. But what?'

I glanced round to be sure that the children weren't listening. 'She knew that I feel bad about Young Murdo. I knew how upset he was and I did nothing about it. I was hiding my feelings, but she knew. I think she's a witch.'

'More than likely,' said Alice.

We had hardly begun to unwind with our drinks when I heard another car arrive. I put my glass on the mantelpiece and returned to the front door. While the Lada ground away towards Easter Coullie, its place had been taken by a Rover, equally elderly but in a much better state of preservation.

Ralph Enterkin, the premier local solicitor, made a controlled exit from the car. He was at least as overweight as Mrs Heminson but his tubby figure somehow managed to bounce up the steps although he was puffing slightly when he arrived at the top. I welcomed him in. I liked the old fellow. Although he did still sometimes treat me as an amusingly alien creature from outer space, I found his pedantic and sometimes grandiloquent manner of speech more nearly familiar than the local dialect. It pleased me and, if it did sometimes infect my writing style, that was easily modified in the next read-through.

He accepted a chair. When I offered him a drink he glanced at his watch, to see that afternoon was on the point of becoming evening, and accepted a glass of his favourite sherry. The children went straight to him. They regarded him as a favourite uncle although, having married late and produced no children of his own, I think that he was secretly terrified of them.

Alice, who had been clearing away the tea-things, smiled a greeting. 'Shall I join you?' she asked.

'For a drink, by all means,' the solicitor said. 'You might care to hear what I have to say, but it may prove unsuitable while these rascals are listening. My words might not be understood but they could be repeated, parrot-fashion.'

'I'll leave you, then.'

'No doubt you will have it all out of your husband before I am out of sight.'

'Long before then,' I said, 'knowing the speed you drive.'

Mr Enterkin looked surprised that anyone should consider him a slow driver when it was an established fact that he was alone in maintaining the ideal speed, the rest of the world's population being dangerous road-hogs. Alice laughed, made a face at me and shooed the children back into the garden.

'I had no wish to encounter the Heminsons here,' Enterkin said, 'so I have been waiting in the distance for their dilapidated vehicle to depart. I shall call on them shortly to pay my respects and to pass on much the same message as I have for yourself – although in the circumstances I suppose that I shall have to cloak it with a degree of circumlocution.'

'You're already cloaking it enough for any circumstances,' I said. 'What might that message be?'

He sipped and then looked at me over his glass. I thought that he looked, for once, embarrassed. 'It is the first time in my long career that I have been engaged for quite so delicate a matter, so I am uncertain how to proceed.' He sighed. 'Best, perhaps, to plunge straight in. Wallace James and Ronnie Fiddler are being beset by the townsfolk for news of events at Easter Coullie. There is, of course, endless speculation in the town.

'You, for your part, are the one person who was present at the finding of both bodies and has also been privy to much of the investigation. I therefore suppose you to be the – ah – person most able to speak with authority and most likely to have credibility if he should happen to disseminate some further information.'

'In other words, spread the gossip,' I said. 'I'll do what I can.'

'Thank you. One rumour presently current seems to be that Mr McKee murdered the Murdo Heminsons Senior and Junior by means unspecified. His motive is generally believed to have been a presumed affair between Murdo Junior and Miss McKee—'

A possibility that had been lurking in my subconscious mind leaped to the surface. 'They think that he put her in the club?'

The solicitor looked at me reprovingly. 'Even the gossip-mongers of the town have so far refrained from phrasing it quite so bluntly. But it has been suggested that the alleged affair has resulted in her pregnancy. The refusal of the boy, at his father's insistence, to acknowledge any responsibility for the matter, would have furnished a motive of sorts – although, in these predominantly agricultural communities and in this day and age, the motive would not be as compelling as once it might have been.

'I have been engaged by Mr McKee both to guard his interests in the matter of any suspicion of having committed the alleged crimes and to defend the reputation of his daughter.'

My mind leaped ahead again. 'I can see why you referred to the matter as delicate,' I said.

'Quite so.'

'My own opinion, for what it's worth, would have been that they were still in the state in which the touch of a hand is magic, a brush of lips the ultimate in amorous adventure.'

'You would have been correct. Or so I would suppose – I have no direct evidence as to the state of their minds and emotions. This morning, Mr McKee summoned one of the family's doctors – the lady member of the practice,' Mr Enterkin said hastily, avoiding my eye, 'to examine Miss McKee.' He glanced at me sideways and saw that I disapproved. 'I agree, a terrible thing to do to the girl, although one can understand his reasons. The outcome was that she was pronounced *virgo intacta* and I have a certificate to that effect which I have shown to Inspector Fellowes, much to his embarrassment.'

'I'll bet. I wish I'd been there to see his face.'

'It would not have given you pleasure. So far so good. But Mr McKee also requires that I quash any rumours presently in circulation. Not the easiest of tasks. One can hardly take out an advertisement in the local paper or put up a card in the post-office, so I rely on you to see that any – um – speculation in that area is firmly quashed.'

'Here!' I said. 'That's a bit of a tall order.'

'But one that you are perfectly capable of implementing.'

'She'll never live it down.'

'I would have thought,' he said mildly, 'that virginity was the state most easily lived down.'

'As you pointed out, this is a different day and age. The modern girl seems to compete to see who can be the first to get rid of it. She'll be a laughing stock. What's more, I can't think of anything more certain to make her dispose of it to the first comer.'

The solicitor, who had clearly not thought along those lines, looked mildly shocked. 'Be that as it may, I rely on you. I must now, with the greatest reluctance but following my client's vehement instructions, go and convey the same information to Mrs Heminson, adding that any suggestion to the contrary would be followed by an action for slander. During her visit here . . . ?'

'Not a word was said about it,' I told him. 'On the contrary, she suggested that the provision of grandchildren would now be Brett's responsibility. She avoided the whole subject of how and why and who.'

'How and why and who what?' Mr Enterkin frowned in irritation and rephrased his question. 'Was she referring to the matter of grandchildren or to the death of her husband?'

'The latter. The McKees were hardly mentioned.'

'I am relieved to hear it. Not that the lady is a gossip, exactly, but who knows how a woman's tongue will run on when she has been wrongfully bereaved? And now I must go.' He got to his feet and put down his empty sherry glass. 'This will not be easy. Perhaps I should have asked for a large brandy instead.'

'It's not too late.'

'No, no. It is, if anything, too early. Thank you, but I must keep an unclouded mind to avoid the pitfalls ahead. My regards to your good lady.'

'And mine to yours,' I replied with equal courtesy. 'You might find her a more useful disseminator of your tidings.'

Mrs Enterkin was usually to be found ornamenting the bar of the hotel while serving behind it.

'You are right. I shall broach the matter shortly.' He returned to his car and drove off, more slowly than ever, in the direction of Easter Coullie.

I went back to the study and completed my narrative, finishing with the solicitor's news. When I sat back and thought about it, the mystery seemed more clouded than ever. Whatever buried memory was tickling the back of my mind still refused to surface. I opened a new reference and began a rough tabulation of what theories remained.

Young Murdo might have taken his own life. Or it was still possible that he had been murdered, perhaps because somebody thought that he had seen too much on the previous day. Whether or not he had in fact seen anything was irrelevant. But surely the police or the forensic scientists would have found traces if he had been manhandled, conscious or unconscious, into his final position.

Miss Mather could almost be dismissed out of hand. She had been angry enough at the time; she might have known where Old Murdo's rifle awaited her use and she would certainly have had humane-killer blanks available, but her possession of airgun pellets was less likely. But Young Murdo had hardly been in a position to witness her crime, nor would her guilt have given him any cause for suicide. There had been no sign of her when he died. Or had she, I wondered, been on Ken McKee's land? The police would know by now. All in all, the lady vet seemed a very unlikely starter.

Much the same arguments applied to Duggie Bracken.

Mrs Heminson just might have killed her husband. All things considered, they had seemed a surprisingly devoted couple. But such impressions are often misleading – a couple who fight like terriers in private will often present an affectionate front to the world. His mother's guilt would certainly have

130

given Young Murdo a motive for suicide. Had she confessed it while he was with her at the hospital? But then who had cleaned the rifle? Brett?

Or had the whole family been in conspiracy?

If the old lady in her upper window was to be believed, Brett was in the clear as far as his father's death was concerned. Unless his place on the tractor had been taken by Young Murdo? But I was sure that the tractor had not come near us during the few minutes before and after Old Murdo's death; and there would have been no time for more complicated movements if both sons were to arrive promptly at the scene of their father's death.

Ken McKee seemed to be alibied for both deaths, but what of his daughter? A young girl driven to distraction by love might well have killed – indeed, many have done so. She could have come over the bridge without being seen from below and have crawled between the rape crop and the hedge with her father's air cane. Her guilt might well have driven Young Murdo to suicide.

Young Murdo himself seemed to have a strong motive for patricide. He had been out of our sight before I started back towards the house. He also could have crawled up between the rape and the hedge and shot his father from the corner of the rape-field. After the deed, and after his quarrel with the girl for whom, presumably, he had committed it, he might well have finished by destroying himself. Alternatively, it was possible that Brett had avenged his father's death. But there remained the fact that Young Murdo had been armed only with a low-powered air rifle. I was sure that once he had removed this and the tin of Cymag from his bag there had been nothing of any size in it.

There had to be another weapon, I realized suddenly. Perhaps an off-certificate .22 rifle or pistol that had been hidden before the deed and probably buried after it.

Or had Young Murdo and the girl conspired? Had she lent

him her father's air cane? Then a quarrel, a threat of exposure and suicide . . . It seemed possible. Indeed, for the first time I found that I had a theory that did not rouse in me an instant reaction of disbelief. And yet I knew, without knowing how I knew, that the memory that still had to surface would not quite fit into that pattern. Almost, but not quite.

I was still trying to assemble these thoughts into some kind of tidy, tabulated form when yet another car halted in front of the house, a door slammed, feet sounded on the steps and I saw Keith Calder's head appear above the rockery.

I was quick enough to meet him on the doorstep. From local accounts, he had been a ladykiller as a young man and had had the sort of good looks that make other men grind their teeth. Now, on the verge of becoming a grandfather, he was taking on the mature handsomeness of the sort of elder statesman who is respected for his ability but elected because the women voters fantasize about him. He had even kept all his hair, a boon which I, who had lost much of mine, frankly envied.

'Molly and I set off as soon as I could get away,' he said. 'Deborah's getting a lift back with an old flame. I came straight to you as the best source of a clear account of whatever it is that's got everybody in a tizzy.'

'I'm flattered,' I said.

'So you should be. Ian's like any other policeman. He'd want to proceed by question and answer and he'd ask all the wrong questions. We could go on for ever. Wal would want to tell me first about the shop and Ronnie becomes incoherent when he gets excited. I look to you as the one person who can spell it out clearly.'

'I've just finished putting all I know and think onto disk,' I told him, indicating the sitting room. 'Have a beer while I print it out.'

He circled round me into the study. As usual he seemed to

crackle with nervous energy. 'No time for that,' he said. 'Molly's expecting me home immediately if not sooner. I'll read it off your monitor. Which disks?'

I showed him the disks. He has a similar word processor to mine and is adept at speed reading, so I left him to it and took a beer out to a chair in the garden and the evening sun. The children, of course, swarmed over me if a pigeon pair can be said to swarm. It certainly felt like swarming. We played a game with no rules, no winners and especially no losers until Alice swept them off for their evening meal.

I gave them ten minutes, which is as long as it takes them to consume any given quantity of food, and I was about to go and offer my help with bath-time when I heard another car.

Alice would be busy. And the evening air was cooler. I quitted my seat in the garden and went through to admit Ian, who was champing on the doorstep.

'Keith's car's here,' he said. 'Where is he?'

Greetings seemed to be going out of fashion, but I wished him a good evening and opened the study door. The screen was blank and Keith was staring raptly out of the window at the scene lit by the low evening sun. Ian tapped his father-in-law on the shoulder. 'I need your help,' he said.

Keith blinked at him. 'Don't you just,' he agreed. 'I've been reading Simon's account. It seems comprehensive. I take it you haven't got any more out of the McKees?'

'The girl's hysterical and the father's sullen. Mrs McKee's gone to bed with a migraine and Ralph Enterkin's standing guard.'

'Well, I don't know what the panic was about,' Keith grumbled. 'I could almost have told you the answer over the phone and had another day and a half at the Game Fair. It all seems very very simple and obvious.'

Ian seethed for a few seconds. 'What does?' he demanded at last. 'If you can figure out what happened, for God's sake tell me.' It would not have done for a rising police officer to grab his own father-in-law and give him a good shaking but I could see that the impulse was there and barely restrained. I could sympathize. Keith can be maddening at times.

Keith gave the scene beyond my window one more penetrating look, as though he suspected it of deliberately hiding something from him, and then shook his head. 'I need a little more time to think about it and make sure that I'm right,' he said. 'After all, you've known most of this for a couple of days and I've only just found out about it. And I want to do a little research and set up a demonstration. There's no hurry. Nothing's going to change. If I prove to you how it could have happened, how it almost certainly did happen, you'll see for yourself how to get the evidence you still need. For the moment, do nothing. You ought to be able to manage that. Masterly inactivity is the forte of the police.'

He looked at his watch. 'I must go. You'll get your wife back about this time tomorrow, Ian; she's shooting for one of the clay pigeon teams. Come to Briesland House tomorrow morning around eleven. You too,' he added to me. 'It'll save me going over it all again for your memoirs.' He rose, called a hail and farewell to Alice and, ignoring Ian's protests, made his departure.

'I suppose he knows what he's doing,' Ian said doubtfully.

'He usually does. Well, I'll see you in the morning.' He headed for the front door.

'Hoy!' I said. 'Where do you think you're going?'

'Home.'

'You're eating here, remember?'

Ian snapped his fingers in irritation. 'I'd forgotten. That bloody man has the knack of driving things out of my mind. Thanks.'

I took him into the sitting room, got him seated and poured him a large drink. I could see him unwinding by the minute now that a solution was within somebody's sight if not his own, so I let him sit in peace. Ian might be infuriated by his father-in-law but he had faith in him.

My own mind had let go of the puzzle at last. Keith had taken over. Just why we should all assume that he would wave a magic wand was uncertain, except that he had often done so in the past. Ian echoed my thought. Suddenly, he laughed.

'How the hell does he do it?' he said.

'A quick mind,' I replied. 'Lateral thinking. And, usually, some fragment of technical information that you and I ought to have known but didn't.'

'That's about it. Although we're not being quite fair to ourselves.' Ian stretched until his joints cracked. 'Those scraps of technical knowledge,' he said musingly, 'usually turn out to be the sort of things I should have been able to find out for myself if I'd gone to the right sources and asked the right questions. All the same, he cuts corners in a way that would land me in front of a disciplinary hearing. Keith's saved my bacon before now, but one of these days it'll be my pleasant duty to lock him up.'

'Deborah won't like that,' I said.

'Only the other day she suggested it.'

I had to admit that I could believe it. 'Can you pick me up in the morning?' I asked. 'Alice wants the car.'

'All right. Be ready or you walk.'

He finished his drink and came up with me to bath the children. It turned into a hilarious event and we both got very wet. Alice came dashing up to read the riot act because water was coming through the kitchen ceiling.

SEVEN

When Ian arrived in the morning he was in a police car complete with a uniformed PC as driver. It seemed unlikely that his rank demanded such a dignified mode of travel, so I assumed at first that he was hoping to make an immediate arrest. I discarded that idea in a hurry when I remembered that I would be the only possible suspect present.

Briesland House dates from about the same mid-Victorian period as Tansy House, but whereas my home was built, soundly and in the local stone but without pretension, for some white-collar worker, perhaps a farm manager or a head gamekeeper, there was no mistaking Briesland House for anything but a Gentleman's Residence. Sited on a slight rise among trees but having a view over the fields to Newton Lauder and beyond, it had a quietly opulent dignity and had been bought, I was told, with the reward paid out by an insurance company. That, somehow, was typical of Keith. I felt a momentary pang of envy. With the family growing, we would soon have to move or extend Tansy House.

It was before eleven when we rolled up the by-road and in through the gates to park on the gravel sweep in front of the house in the shade of a large sycamore. We left the constable waiting patiently behind the wheel.

We found Keith occupying one of the several deckchairs set out in more shade at the side of the house, a favourite sitting spot of Keith and his family. There was coffee on the table. Another table some yards away in the sunlight supported an assortment of weapons and a pair of binoculars.

'You seem to have been busy,' I said as we settled in deckchairs. 'Have we missed anything?'

'Not a damn thing,' Keith said. He poured coffee for both of us. 'I'm almost as curious as you are and I was tempted to start my tests, but there was no point if I was going to have to do it all again to convince you.'

Ian was nodding. 'So who's the guilty party?'

'All in good time. Your murderer isn't going anywhere, I guarantee it.'

I thought that Ian would protest, but he knew his father-in-law. He sighed and gave way. 'Do I need a man to take notes?' he asked.

'We're not at that stage yet. If you're satisfied with a preliminary demonstration this morning, I'll do some properly monitored tests and give you a precognition. And if I should happen to want a witness as to what were my exact words, to prevent the wicked police twisting them, Simon's good at that.' He looked at me approvingly. 'Your account of what happened included, and quite rightly, some very interesting details plus almost every word everybody said – and very revealing some of them proved!'

'But my comments on the possible suspects? I suppose that they were garbage, as usual?'

'As a matter of fact, not. At least after you'd got past havering on about nail-guns and humane killers – what idiot put that idea into your head?' he asked Ian.

'As you say, an idiot,' Ian said without looking at me. 'I'm not naming names.'

'Just as well. After that, your summary kept heading in the right direction,' Keith told me, 'and then veering away. You just didn't go far enough. Are we ready?'

Ian pointed out that he had been more than ready for some little time. I drained my coffee cup and we got up. Keith led us to the other table.

The garden of Briesland House features small lawns and grass walks which wander among the trees and shrubs to charming effect. A pigeon was calling, somewhere overhead. The other table had been carefully placed so that a vista stretched for about forty yards to the high stone wall that surrounded the property. At the wall, a tall plank had been erected. It seemed to have been marked with a row of dots down the centre-line, like buttons on a guardsman's tunic.

Short of the table, Keith halted us. 'You two bide there,' he said, 'behind the firing line, while I give you my short course on what various weapons can and can't do. You'd better have this at your fingertips, Ian, for discussions with the Procurator Fiscal and in case you're ever asked about it in court.

'First, the conventional two-two rifle. Fit only for controlling rabbits and the like, despite the fuss the police make about it. Almost a child's toy, but Ronnie was correct; in careless hands it can kill at a considerable distance if it happens to find the right spot – or the wrong one, depending on which way round you're looking at it. You still have the Heminsons' rifle, Ian, so this is the nearest I could put my hands on. I'll take the top aiming mark.'

Taking up a small, single-shot rifle that I had sometimes seen him use on rabbits, he loaded and fired five times in succession, the sharp cracks echoing back off the house and the garden walls. I saw splinters fly. Birdsong was cut off and the pigeon rattled out of a treetop and flew away.

Ian was watching through the binoculars. 'Nice group,' he said.

'I could do better with an elbow rest,' Keith said, 'but it'll do. That's an oak board, almost an inch thick. I'm guessing that it would offer about the same resistance as the thicker part of a skull. Maybe not exactly, but about the same order of magnitude. Produce a few skulls for me – fresh ones, not skulls that have dried out – and I'll do it all again for evidence.'

'Not a chance,' Ian said.

'One would do at a pinch. I'd expect all those shots to have gone clean through the board. D'you want to go and look?'

Ian lowered the binoculars. 'They've penetrated all right. We'll take a closer look later.'

Keith put down the rifle and picked up what seemed to be an ordinary if cumbersome walking-stick. 'This is an air cane by Reilly,' he said. 'Unfortunately, this and the next gun are held as antiques. It would be quite illegal for me to fire either of them.' He paused and looked vaguely into the distance.

'Never mind that,' Ian said impatiently. 'I won't tell anybody if you don't. Just this once,' he added.

'Of course,' Keith agreed. 'This air cane is straight, but they were often made with a strange-looking double bend, to make aiming easier. The pump's separate, but once pumped up to around four hundred pounds the square inch you can get off a dozen or more shots before the pressure falls away. That's a lot of hard pumping, I may tell you. I'd have taken it down to the garage this morning and used the air hose, but if the reservoir's weakened by corrosion you can destroy an old air cane by using a compressor. The alternative is pure sweat. I nearly phoned for you to send along a couple of beefy constables to give me a hand.'

'You knew in advance that I would tell you to break the law,' Ian said.

'Of course. This was made for Number Two Bore, equivalent to two-two.'

Keith dropped an airgun pellet through the loading hole and took up a small gadget from the table. 'It requires the use of a cocking key,' he explained. As he turned the key there was a sharp click and a stud popped up at about the mid-point. He raised the stick, sighted along it and fired by pressing the stud with his left thumb.

Ian had the binoculars up again. 'You're off to the right,' he said.

'That's usual with a stud trigger. This time I'm in no doubt whatever that the slug would have gone through several thicknesses of board.' Repeating the same steps, he fired another four slugs into the target board. The sound was sharper but lighter than that of the conventional rifle.

'Not such a good group,' Ian said.

'Well, it wouldn't be. The cranked sticks are more accurate because you can shoot from the shoulder, but the shape must have been a giveaway for a poacher. If you think that you can do better, have a go.'

'Thank you,' Ian said, 'but no. If you're trying to convince me that an air cane could have been used to kill Old Murdo—'

'Could,' Keith said. 'Not that it did.'

'Oh. Anyway, you've succeeded,' Ian finished doggedly. I suppressed a sigh as my favourite theory vanished into thin air.

'And our next little item,' Keith said. He picked up a gun that resembled the flintlock fowling pieces that figured largely in his collection, but with a metal sphere slightly larger than a tennis ball fitted in front of the trigger guard. 'I'd have liked to fire this one for you, but I won't. Seventeenth century, maker unknown. The ones with a copper air reservoir are comparatively safe – the reservoir fails by splitting if it fails at all – but when an iron ball like this fails it goes off like a grenade.'

'If somebody had been lugging a thing like that around, he'd have been noticed,' Ian said.

'Very true. And for my next trick . . .' Keith laid down the antique and picked up an unusually shaped modern gun. 'A pump-up air rifle by Crossman. I imported it for the keeper at

143

Horsefield Great House and I've borrowed it back from him. He likes it for vermin control because it's comparatively quiet and the ammunition's cheap. Well above the permitted power, so he holds it on his Firearms Certificate.'

'Now, just a minute,' Ian said sharply. 'I looked through our computer records and I didn't see it.'

'I can't help that. It's on his certificate or I wouldn't have sold it to him. One of your clerks in the Firearms Department probably thought the keeper was being over-meticulous. "Airgun," he thought to himself and he didn't bother transferring it to the record.'

'I'll have his balls for bools,' Ian said. (Bools, I knew, were boy's marbles – the word almost certainly coming from the French.) 'He isn't paid to think. Go on.'

'Next aiming mark.' Keith worked a bolt which incorporated a sliding sleeve, loaded a pellet and fired. I thought that the noise was less than that of the air cane. 'Muzzle velocity about six hundred and fifty feet per second,' he said. 'The Sheridan gets up to nearly eight hundred. But that's against about five-fifty for the ordinary spring-operated boy's airgun. Not a hell of a difference when you remember that the quicker it's moving the faster it decelerates.' He loaded and fired several more shots. 'There are more powerful gas-operated air weapons, but I don't know of any in this neck of the woods. I doubt if any of these shots have gone all the way through.'

Ian peered through the binoculars. 'They haven't,' he said. 'Beautiful group, though.'

'Thank you. It's the sudden uncoiling of the spring that throws an ordinary airgun all over the place. Pump-ups don't have that problem. Back to the two-two rifle.' Keith made the substitution. 'Waisted airgun pellet and blank cartridge.' Keith fired two shots, each time dropping a pellet into the breech and pushing it home with the brass cartridge. 'Those were with dummy-launcher blanks. Next the "Green", three-grain cartridge for the humane killer . . . now nail-gun blanks . . . and finally just plain blank cartridges as used in a shotgun adaptor for dog-tests. How's that?'

With the naked eye I could see that the middle of the target board seemed to have been attacked by deathwatch beetle. Ian lowered the binoculars. 'Not a good group,' he said. 'Some of them keyholed and I think that only one of them went all the way through.'

'We'll take a look in a minute,' Keith said. 'I'd expect you to be right.'

'But which one of those represents what Old Murdo's killer really did?' Ian asked.

'None of them.'

Ian drew in his breath in an impatient hiss. 'Then why are we wasting my time and a lot of expensive ammunition – for which no doubt you will expect to be reimbursed—?'

'You sound more like your super every day,' Keith said. 'You're going to have to sell the explanation to your highheid-yins, the Procurator Fiscal, the Sheriff and probably a jury, so I wanted you to have an idea of the comparisons. Some prat's bound to start asking awkward questions to get his name in the papers, and you want to be able to show that you've been as thorough as anybody could have been.'

He put down the rifle and picked up the last weapon. 'Now to the common or garden, low-powered air rifle. This is Young Murdo's, recovered from the shop this morning.' Keith cocked it by levering down the hinged barrel, dropped in a pellet and fired. The lower velocity was evident from the softer sound and the delay before the pellet rapped into the board. Keith loaded and fired four more times in quick succession.

'Now watch,' he said, reloading. He added a few drops from a Three-in-One oil tin. 'This oil was in Young Murdo's bag, which Ronnie picked up.' When he fired, the slap of the pellet followed too quickly to be distinguished from the loud crack

145

of the shot. I was not ready for it and I jumped.

Ian raised the binoculars. 'You're low,' he said. 'But it certainly went clean through. I can see daylight. What in God's name did you do?'

'Let's take a look,' Keith said. He laid down the air rifle with as much care as if he had been handling a Best London shotgun and we walked forward. The oak plank was well riddled with holes. The earlier shots from Young Murdo's air rifle had penetrated but the skirts of the pellets were still visible. When Keith turned the plank round, the lower shot could be seen to have punched a large splinter out of the reverse side on its exit.

'It's called "diesel action",' Keith said. 'The ordinary airgun uses thin air, compressed by one mechanical action or another, to propel the pellet. Sometimes an airgun gets over-lubricated with a light oil. And some users put a drop of oil behind the pellet to give it both lubrication and a good seal. If the action is already warm, the oil can vaporize. When the gun's fired, the compression in the air chamber shoots the temperature straight up to around eight hundred degrees centigrade. That's quite enough to ignite the oil vapour and produce a considerable rise in pressure.'

I listened intently to Keith's words. My memory had at last thrown up an incident in my boyhood and I could see how Keith's story was going to end.

Ian studied both sides of the plank in silence. 'Why did it shoot low?' he asked at last.

Keith shrugged. 'Possibly what's known as muzzle-flip. More probably, the extra pressure caused the barrel to pivot slightly downward in a beginning of the reloading action.'

'So Old Murdo's death . . . ?'

'Was accidental. Young Murdo was furious with his father. He needed to blow off steam and at the same time he wanted to give the old man a fright. Simon noted how dusty he was.

If you still have the clothes he was wearing, you'll probably find that the dust is clay soil and rape-seed, not the sandy stuff down in the gully. He crawled along between the rape crop and the hedge and fired from the corner, as he thought, over his father's head. But he'd given his air rifle, which had been in a hot sun all morning, a little more oil. The result was a very powerful shot, some inches lower than his point of aim. The old man fell but, at the time, Young Murdo probably thought that he'd fainted. He may have thought, or even half hoped, that he'd provoked a heart attack.

'When he realized that he'd shot his father, Young Murdo was scared to say anything. He was horrified. Over the next twenty-four hours it sank in. He knew that he'd killed his father. The old man might have been a cantankerous old cuss threatening his son's romance, but he was also the sheet-anchor of the family. The poor lad never knew that his father had a brain-tumour that was going to carry him off anyway. On top of all that, the effect of that particular shot would be a mystery to him. It must have seemed like the work of the evil genie haunting him. Something had happened that he couldn't understand and that he was sure nobody, especially the incredulous Inspector Fellowes, was going to believe.

'I think you'll find that Sheila McKee had seen something from the knoll. She hadn't seen it all, but enough to make her wonder. I suggest that you put it to her through Ralph Enterkin; she'll come clean.

'Sheila McKee broke off with Young Murdo and that proved to be the last straw. He went back to the rabbit-holes, sprinkled some water, followed it up with Cymag, stuck his head inside and took a deep breath.'

Ian stooped and fingered the exit hole. 'Accident followed by suicide,' he said. 'You'll give me a precognition covering the technical part of this?'

'As soon as I've carried out some more tests. I'd want to

147

be able to quote figures about penetration, just in case the Procurator Fiscal has any doubts.'

Ian stood, rubbing his neck, for a full minute. 'I'd better get back,' he said. 'I'll have to call off the other enquiries and report to my chiefs.' He walked off towards his car and then stopped and looked back. 'Thanks,' he said.

'Any time,' said Keith.

Ian nodded and walked on.

'You could give me a hand with this table, if you insist,' Keith said.

The table was only a light card-table but the weight of the guns turned it into an awkward burden. We carried it to the French windows. Ian was waiting impatiently at the corner of the house, beyond earshot.

'I think you should come over and tell me a little more,' I said quietly.

'Damned if I do.'

'Yes, you will,' I said. I took the Three-in-One tin off the table. Keith checked a quick movement of his hand. I dropped the tin into my pocket and caught up with Ian at the car.

Ian seemed to be preoccupied during the journey, but he roused himself once to sniff the air. 'What's that smell?' he asked.

'I can't smell anything,' I said.

The house, when Ian dropped me at the foot of the steps, was empty except for lonely echoes. Alice had left me something in the microwave oven. I heated it up and ate it before heading for the study. Otherwise, I knew, it would be congealed on the plate the next time I saw it.

I always think better in front of my word processor, where thoughts can be assembled and pushed around until they make sense. I toyed half-heartedly with my problem. I knew that Keith would come and, sure enough, in mid-afternoon I recognized the sound of his jeep. I had left the doors open and when he reached the threshold I called to him to come in.

He entered the study with the caution of an animal nosing a trap, ignoring the chair that awaited him. 'Is Alice at home?' he asked.

'She's taken the babes to visit her aunt in Kirkcaldy. That's why I suggested that we meet here. We have privacy.'

'What did you want to talk about?'

'Sit or stand,' I said. 'It's all the same to me. That was a load of rubbish you sold Ian, wasn't it?'

Keith sat down slowly. 'I don't know what you mean,' he said.

'Yes, you do.' I held up the Three-in-One oil can. Without Ian's presence he could make a proper grab for it, but I was too quick for him. I dropped it into a desk drawer, out of his reach.

'Give me that,' he said.

'Certainly not. It's evidence. Not that it would make any difference if you grabbed it and drank it, except to your insides. Ian noticed the smell in the car. I'd only have to remind him. You faked the whole thing, didn't you? Do you really think a sheriff's inquiry will go along with it?'

'I don't see why not,' he said defiantly. 'Accident and suicide. A very satisfactory verdict from everybody's point of view. Why don't you like it?'

I may not know much about guns,' I said, 'but I know you better than Ian does and I can usually tell when you're . . . dissembling, to put it nicely.'

'You bastard,' he said, more in anger than sorrow. 'Almost every word I told Ian was the truth. Tell me what you think doesn't fit.'

'So that you can polish up your version?' I was beginning to enjoy myself. It is not often that I can argue with Keith successfully. I refreshed my memory with a glance at the monitor. 'For a start, I had an airgun when I was a boy. I used to lubricate it generously. One day I was shooting at a milk bottle full of water that I'd put on the sundial on the lawn. My shots were just bouncing off it. But my third or fourth shot went off like the crack of doom. The bottle shattered and for a moment there was a rainbow hanging in the air. The rainbow in the spray when Jean Mather was using the power-hose on her car almost reminded me of it, but not quite.'

'There you are,' Keith said. 'You've proved my point.'

'But it only happened once out of all my shots. You read my notes. I noted down that Young Murdo shot a rabbit at about twenty yards and boasted that he could kill them dead at three times the range. That means that he could produce a powerful shot whenever he wished. But if the pressure kicked the barrel down, he couldn't possibly connect with a rabbit regularly at long range.'

'He could probably prevent that happening by keeping a good grip on the barrel,' Keith said, too quickly.

'You think so? But again, I was standing right behind you when you fired that last shot. I thought at the time that you dropped your aim.'

'And is that all?'

'Not by a mile. You skated rather evasively around the question of heat. By the time Young Murdo came to fire at or over his father, it must have been many minutes since his last shot. And he'd been crawling along in the shade of a hedge. His airgun would be barely warm.

'Then there was the disturbance at the corner of the rape-field. From what Ian said, I gathered that it must be about where Young Murdo would have dropped his gear when he ran to join us beside his father's body. Maybe he was con-cerned about a cheap airgun or the tin of Cymag, but I don't think that he was looking for either of those. What's so special about that oil-tin that doesn't smell like oil?' When he hesitated, I added, 'I've got more than enough to write it up already.'

'But you wouldn't,' he said. He bit his lip and then made up his mind. 'All right. Promise me that you won't say or write any of this while they're still in the neighbourhood?'

'I promise.'

He sighed. 'Sniff it,' he said.

'I already sniffed. Whatever it is, it isn't Three-in-One oil,' I said. 'The smell took me back, but I can't place it.'

'Something much more volatile than Three-in-One oil,' Keith said. 'I'm fairly sure that it's model aircraft fuel. With something like that in the works, a spring airgun will diesel almost every time – and with more power than gun-oil would give it. If you want an airgun to diesel on a light lubricating oil like Three-in-One, you usually have to fire it first without a pellet, to get the oil heated and vaporized, and then fire it again with a pellet up the spout. Happy now?'

'I wouldn't claim to be happy. I don't like it much. But at least it's the truth at last. Isn't it?'

Keith nodded. 'Ian fell into the trap and I hope he stays there. Sometimes I worry for the intelligence of any grand-children Deborah gives me. A policeman should be seeking the truth, not just a solution.'

My conclusions were falling into place. 'So Young Murdo did deliberately shoot his father. The McKee girl, from her haunt on the knoll, saw him go sneaking off in the direction of the farmhouse. She broke off with him, which pushed him over the edge.'

'But,' Keith said, 'when Ian goes to question her again and suggests an accident, she'll speak up. She may have been horrified by what she suspected, but he was still her first love. My guess is that she's been holding her tongue rather than accuse the dead boy of murder as well as suicide.'

'Which is pretty much what we're doing,' I pointed out.

151

'So it is. The thing is, Bertha Heminson may be a tough old boot, and she may look like one of the witches in *Macbeth* who's been overdoing it on the poisoned entrails, but I like her. And Brett's a good lad. Why bring more scandal down on them when it won't serve any purpose? There's no culprit alive to be brought to book.'

I was surprised to find myself in full agreement with him. 'And there's the girl,' I said.

'Yes. Of course, she may know about his trick with the model aeroplane fuel. I had a word with Ralph Enterkin as soon as you left Briesland House. He's of the same mind. He's going to make sure that she holds her wheesht about that.'

So far, I thought, so good. 'But you'll fall on your face if the court wants you to demonstrate,' I told him.

'It won't happen. Courts in this country go by what expert witnesses tell them, not by seeing for themselves. I think it's because of a slavish devotion to the written record.'

One point still worried me. 'Sheila McKee must have guessed that the boy committed murder and suicide over her,' I said. 'She'll be devastated. Any girl would.'

Keith looked at me pityingly. 'That shows how little you know about women,' he said. He picked up my late uncle's binoculars, which stood in their usual place beside my bird-book by the window, and focused them. 'Most of them would boast about it for the rest of their lives. But not young Sheila. She's an honest lassie.' Keith looked round at me again before deciding to say more. 'She reminds me a little of Deborah at the same age. A trusting nature but a hard core of common sense. And she doesn't have to prove that she can attract the young men.' He handed me the binoculars and pointed. 'I think she'll be all right.'

I got up, refocused the binoculars and looked where he indicated. On top of the knoll I could see the small, seated figure of the girl. She was in shade but silhouetted against sunlit grass, leaning back against the trunk of a small silver birch. Leaning against the same tree was another figure. Carefully adjusting the focus, I recognized Brett.

In the distance, the girl turned her head to look at the young man. I had seen the same movement when she looked back at Young Murdo on the day of the first death. It had seemed familiar at the time and I had seen it again only a few minutes earlier. The proud carriage of the head was unmistakable.

'Why are you going to so much trouble?' I asked him suddenly. 'You're covering up a murder and you're prepared to go before a sheriff and twist the truth on oath.'

'I told you—'

'You told me a load of rubbish,' I said. 'You may like young Brett, but Bertha Heminson is a long way from being your sort of person. It's the girl, isn't it?'

When he tried very hard to look both innocent and indignant, I knew that I had the whole story at last. 'What are you suggesting?' he demanded.

'That she's your daughter,' I said.

'You're out of your skull,' he said more quietly.

'It's strange that you should mention skulls,' I told him. 'Both Mr and Mrs McKee have short necks and round skulls like Christmas puddings. Sheila's quite different. She has a longer skull, set higher, and when she turns her head to look behind her she reminds me very much of you. Does Molly know?'

He hesitated and then nodded.

'I've already promised you that I wouldn't write the story as long as the Heminsons were in the district. I'll make the same promise in respect of the McKees.'

'My reputation, of course, doesn't matter a damn?'

'Your reputation would remain unchanged,' I pointed out.

He pulled a face but I could see that he was not wholly displeased. 'I never meant it to happen,' he said, 'but I rather think that she did. She always had more than her share of feminine charm but she'd never looked at any other man but Kennie McKee. Then, one day, when I'd had a dram or two, she gave me the come-on. That's not the sort of invitation I've always turned down . . . more fool me. She told me that she was on the pill, but I've often suspected that she knew by then that she and Ken would never have a family together.'

'Does Ken know?'

'I'm sure of it. And I'll tell you something else. Every year I get a Christmas card from Sheila. What do you make of that?'

I opened the drawer and gave him the tin of oil. 'You'll take a dram?' I asked him.

'That's the other invitation I've never had the strength of mind to refuse,' he said.

AUTHOR'S NOTE

At first I was in some doubt as to whether this book should be written. After consideration, however, I decided that I had already offered the reader too many unlikely but, I hope, ingenious methods of murder for one more to matter. Diesel action in airguns is already mentioned in airgun literature.

In researching the various subjects I was greatly helped by Geoff Boothroyd, who not only furnished me with back copies of articles but went to the trouble of testing the blank cartridge/airgun pellet combination; Messrs Accles and Shelvoke Ltd, the manufacturers of humane killers; my local vets, Messrs Williamson and Duncan MSRCVS; and Derrick J. Pounder, Professor of Forensic Medicine at the University of Dundee.

G.H.